"You and I have links from the past."

Drew went on expressionlessly. "Admit it, Charlotte. Like it or not, your father was a close friend of mine."

She pushed her chair back violently. "Oh, I admit it, Drew. There was a time when I was shortsighted enough to put you on a pedestal! You were everything I ever dreamed of being—taking off on your own, single-handedly delivering yachts around the world. You had all the freedom that goes with being a male!"

Drew's eyes were glittery, amused beneath half-closed lids.

"There's nothing to stop females from being as adventurous as males, if they want it badly enough. But I recall something else you wanted, Charlotte," he said softly, tauntingly, "and that had nothing to do with dreaming of being a boy!"

Rosalie Ash, an English writer, abandoned her first intended career for marriage, then worked as a personal secretary for the managing director of a group of building and leisure companies. She stopped work to have her first child and now has two daughters. Somehow, during the hectic days and broken nights, first days at school and ferrying to and from various lessons, Brownies and so on, her new writing career emerged. After a lifelong compulsion to write—and numerous secret scribblings—she finally achieved her ambition to write romance novels. Other pleasures she and her family enjoy are regular visits to the Royal Shakespeare Theatre, entertaining friends, country walks, reading, films and travel.

UNSAFE HARBOUR
Rosalie Ash

Harlequin Books

TORONTO • NEW YORK • LONDON
AMSTERDAM • PARIS • SYDNEY • HAMBURG
STOCKHOLM • ATHENS • TOKYO • MILAN

Original hardcover edition published in 1990
by Mills & Boon Limited

ISBN 0-373-17087-4

Harlequin Romance first edition June 1991

UNSAFE HARBOUR

CHAPTER ONE

CHARLOTTE sat in silence, her fingers linked tightly round her father's thin, motionless hand, her eyes wide with apprehension as she studied his sleeping face. She was trying very hard to transmit positive, constructive thoughts, to *will* him to live. But her mind seemed filled instead with mundane, random thoughts, darting from one to another. The mounting problems at the boatyard, the abruptness of leaving her job in London, the inevitability of bumping into Drew again, now that she was back in Shalmouth.

Her father was unlikely to recover consciousness, the doctor had told her. But it all seemed unreal to Charlotte. A week ago, he'd been propped up in bed, talking to her. True, he'd rambled slightly, mumbling incoherently about the boatyard and the past. But he couldn't possibly be about to die. The last conversation they'd had, there'd been something important he had wanted to tell her, but he'd drifted off again, and the next time she had visited he'd sunk into a coma. The minor frustration of not knowing what he'd been going to say was almost as agonising as the prospect of his actually leaving her forever. She kept telling herself how tanned and fit he looked. He looked much too well to be lying there in a hospital bed, silently slipping further and further away from her. But the private side-ward, the drip strapped to his arm, and his slow, laboured breathing were the subtle pointers to reality, the signs that the worst really could happen.

'*Please* don't die, Dad. . .*please* wake up!' she whispered urgently, pressing his hand with trembling fingers. The door opened quietly behind her, and Fiona tapped her on the shoulder.

'Come on, Charlie. There's no point sitting here for hours on end! The sister said it's only a matter of time. . .and it's no good making yourself ill! Dad wouldn't want that, would he?'

'I know. . .' Charlotte got stiffly to her feet, conscious suddenly of a pain between her shoulder-blades from her hours of vigilance, and scanned her sister's composed face with a valiant effort at a smile. As the elder of the two, she felt perhaps she should be setting an example of stoical acceptance. Yet ironically, Fiona seemed far calmer, far less affected by the very real possibility of their dad's death. Maybe it was because Fee had always been much closer to their mother, Charlotte reflected thoughtfully, glancing over her shoulder at her father's sleeping form as they left the room together. After the shock of their parents' divorce, three years ago, allegiances had been forced unnaturally into the open.

'Let's have a cup of tea together, before I go back up and sit with him,' Fiona was saying, steering Charlotte out of the lift. 'I've been valuing houses all afternoon and I'm exhausted! Come to that, you don't look exactly bouncing with energy yourself!'

'I keep wondering if it's all my fault,' Charlotte confessed awkwardly, facing her sister across a table in the hospital cafeteria. 'I can't stop thinking if only. . .'

'Precisely how can it be your fault?' Fiona demanded in astonishment, lowering her teacup in mid-sip. 'Dad had been ill for ages, apparently, and didn't tell us. Then he slipped off a ladder and hit his head on a two-tonne keel, darling! While you were two hundred miles away in London lugging large bits of antique furniture around!'

'He always wanted me to stay in Shalmouth,' Charlotte pointed out quietly, staring at the thin swirls of steam rising from the hot liquid in her cup. 'If I'd stayed and helped him in the boatyard, I'd have noticed how he was—seen the signs. . .he was obviously in no fit state to be working at all!'

Just talking to Dad on the phone every week hadn't been enough, she realised now, as she drank some of the tasteless tea. She'd certainly never suspected he was hiding a fight against an illness which, according to their GP, would have been increasingly attacking his memory and his sense of balance. If he'd occasionally sounded unhappy, on the other end of the line, she'd put that down to their mother's death the year before. He'd still cared deeply about her. The divorce, coming after so many years of marriage, had rocked his self-confidence terribly, she knew.

It had rocked hers, as well. Her parents had never precisely seen eye to eye, but somehow she'd taken it for granted they'd made their marriage secure. For a while afterwards she'd even found herself wondering guiltily if the constant arguments over her tomboyish inclinations, her fierce championing of her father, and her blatant wish to work in the boatyard could have been the cause of the divorce. This guilt complex waxed and waned, depending on the state of her morale, and during confident moods she could tell herself logically that, after all, she'd opted for another kind of career altogether long before their break-up. She'd gone away to university, gained a degree in fine arts, and got her foot on the ladder of a promising career as a valuer with a famous auction house in London. Albeit for all the wrong reasons, she reminded herself, thinking of the long list of 'if only's she'd been mulling over upstairs at her father's bedside.

What it all came down to, if she was brutally honest, was cowardice. Admit it, she urged herself ruthlessly. She'd turned her back on the boatyard, visited home as infrequently as possible, for the deplorable, spineless reason that she might meet up with Drew again. . . She let out a shaky sigh and sipped some more tea, appalled at this blinding flash of understanding. The imminent death of someone you loved very much seemed to be a powerful catalyst for soul-searching, she acknowledged silently. When she began to analyse things, there appeared to be quite a lot she could blame on Drew

Meredith, and the joke was that the man in question was no doubt blissfully unaware of the far-reaching effect he'd had on her life so far!

Well, she'd been back in Shalmouth a month now, and she was here for good. She'd initially only taken a week off from her job as a porter with Christie's, when she'd heard about Dad's accident, and she'd come down to see what she could do to help. But once she'd spoken to her father, and seen the state of the boatyard business, she'd made up her mind to stay. Dad needed her help. He'd told her so. He'd been so relieved to hear that she'd taken over the reins at the boatyard, she had finally understood how much it meant to him. True, she wasn't the son he'd always longed for, but she was the next best thing. Maybe it would still be possible for Wells Boats to carry on into a third generation of the family, after all.

And facing Drew was just another hurdle to be crossed. There would be nothing to it. A polite nod, a smile of recognition. Five years was a long time. Drew would have forgotten all about the humiliating episode between them, by now.

'I've been in Shalmouth all the time!' Fiona was protesting indignantly, jolting her out of her reverie. 'I hope you're not suggesting I've neglected Dad?'

Charlotte shook her head quickly, her eyes widening in dismay at her sister's offended expression.

'Of course that's not what I meant, darling! I meant if I'd been working with him, he couldn't have hidden his illness from me. I'd have noticed how forgetful he was getting. . .Geoff Bates says he never knew what to expect from one day to the next. He told me Dad had been getting gradually worse ever since Mum died. I'm furious with him for not contacting me months ago, and telling me how things were! The boatyard office work was chaotic. I didn't even know where to begin! I'm still not sure I'm doing the right thing, half the time!'

'I think you're crazy to think you can even try,' Fiona stated bluntly. 'I can't believe you've quit your job in London, with this hare-brained notion of running Wells Boats! Dad may have taught you a lot of things in the past, but you've been away for five years, and things have changed a bit since then. It'll have to be sold, of course,' she added cruelly. 'That's if you *can* sell a boatyard that's not making any money?'

Charlotte carefully replaced her cup in its saucer, avoiding her sister's cool blue gaze. She was well aware that Fiona was deliberately being contentious, because she'd offended her, and sighed. She felt too drained of energy to smooth ruffled feathers. Besides, she knew Fiona. Underneath the brittle exterior was a mass of insecurities and a desperate need for approval. But they'd always been so different, physically and mentally. Charlotte propped her chin on her hand, and reflected on the amazement everyone displayed whenever they revealed they were sisters.

Fiona was so like their mother, in that her character belied her appearance. Petite and rounded, soft and feminine-looking, but with a brisk, no-nonsense attitude to everything and a great impatience for what she called 'foolish sentiment'. Whereas Charlotte supposed she was more like Dad—a bit of a dreamer really, tall, and slim-hipped, her cloud of dark curls a vivid foil for Fiona's fluffy blonde waves.

Draining her cup, she stood up with an attempt at a smile. 'Susie said she'd give me a lift home. I'll have a quick rest and be back by eleven. . .do you mind?'

'No, you get off home. But I've got to go out at eight, so I'll only be able to stay an hour. . .'

Charlotte stared at her sister blankly, as her meaning sank in. 'Fee, *must* you go out tonight?'

The blonde girl shrugged, colour touching her creamy complexion. 'For heaven's sake, Charlie, aren't you playing the martyr? Dad's in hospital, surrounded by nursing staff, not lying at home alone! Sitting up all night is stretching the boundaries of civilised behaviour, if you want my opinion. They'll ring us if anything happens.'

'You don't have to sit up all night with him. I'm only asking you to stay with him until I get back.' She fought to keep her voice level and reasonable.

'But I've got a business meeting! You're just being silly!'

Charlotte drew a deep, steadying breath. 'I accept I'm probably being silly. . .' she shrugged, reaching for her blue waxed jacket to sling on over her denims

'. . .but since Dad's been in this coma, I'm frightened he might die at any moment. . . I just can't bear to think of that happening when he's among strangers.'

She turned to leave quickly, before Fiona could see the mortifying tears stinging the back of her eyes.

A strong wind with a spatter of rain in it whipped her cloudy dark curls across her face as she emerged from the swing-doors, and glanced around for Susie's car. The forecast had been for severe storms, approaching hurricane force. There was the strong tang of salt in the wind as it howled around the corner of the building, and she imagined the sea surging furiously up the estuary and flooding the shed in the small creek behind the boatyard buildings, the gale ripping the canvas covers from the yachts in the storage pen.

She shivered, turning up her collar and scanning the ranks of parked cars, quelling her overactive imagination. Hopefully the main premises would stand up to any weather the February gales could fling at them. Wells Boats had been housed in the same three-storey stone building since 1875. Her grandfather had built huge wooden sailing ships there, before steel had taken over and they'd adapted to smaller wooden boats. A hundred years of withstanding the onslaught of the south-westerly winds should be sufficient reassurance, she decided firmly. She'd been away from the sea too long, in the claustrophobic protection of a big city. She'd forgotten how rough the weather could get on the coast, in the winter.

A horn sounded, and Susie's small yellow Renault drove up in front of her.

'Hop in! This is the Shalmouth Taxi Service!'

Charlotte flopped gratefully into the passenger seat, and smiled at the other girl. 'Thanks, Susie. What I'd do without a friend like you I can't begin to imagine.'

Susie pushed a bright strand of copper-brown hair behind her ear, and grinned, lively brown eyes scanning Charlotte's pallor with a professional air. 'If I was a really good friend, I'd be insisting you had a week of square meals and early nights, not conniving in your effort to grind yourself into the ground!'

'Don't you start! I've just had a lecture from Fiona along similar lines.' Charlotte sighed, leaning back and closing her eyes. It was a gigantic effort to stay awake against the motion of the car.

'Don't worry—I'm so pleased you're back in Shalmouth, I'd do anything for you!' Susie assured her cheerfully. 'But as a trained nurse, I should warn you that you can't go on like this much longer.'

'I doubt if I'll have to,' Charlotte replied quietly. 'The doctor said it could be just a matter of days, even hours. . .'

'Then you must come home with me, darling! I'll cook you a meal, and you can have a rest,' Susie insisted, frowning in concern. 'You can't go back to that lonely little basement flat on your own!'

'I appreciate the offer. But I'd rather be alone, if you don't mind. I'm not meaning to sound martyr-like. I'll have a proper meal,' she added, with a smile, 'but the hospital might ring, and I want to be there if they do. And I've got some thinking to do— I've been mulling over the problems at the boatyard, and I think I might have some good ideas for the future.'

'Things aren't quite as bad there as you thought, then?'

'Oh, they're bad enough! Dad seems to have wound the business down to a spot of maintenance and repair in the autumn, and winter storage. He's let the boat-building and the sail-making side go completely. The frustrating thing is we've still got the biggest premises of any of the boat-builders in Shalmouth. And we should capitalise on our repu-tation as the oldest established! We've got the capacity for building at least four or five new dinghies a year, as well as tackling something gran-der—something that would give Wells Boats back its reputation. And I met someone in the pub one lunchtime last week who could be our salvation,' she finished up, warming to her theme. 'Someone who's designed his own forty-foot racing trimaran for the next Westwind single-handed transatlantic, and he's looking for a small, local boatyard to build it for him. If I can only get the financial side sorted out, I'm positive we could do it!'

'Well, if enthusiasm was the remedy for Wells Boats, your problems would be over! And you sound very knowledgeable, considering you've only been back a month,' Susie remarked, with a slant of her eyebrow.

'I've never lost interest in the boatyard,' Charlotte admitted, with a slight grin. 'I think maybe the sea and boats have always been "in my blood"! Sounds melodramatic, doesn't it?'

'Not when you consider your father and your grandfather,' Susie mused. 'What puzzles me is why you decided to leave Shalmouth in the first place. I've always thought your career in London sounded incredibly exciting, yet at the first sign of trouble here you throw it all up and come charging back. So your heart could never have been in it!'

'No. . .' Charlotte's agreement was vague, and she adroitly changed the subject, asking after Susie's spirited twin boys and laughing at their reported antics.

'Drop me by Paxtons Garage, could you?' she suggested, as they drove through the centre of the town. Her finances didn't stretch to her own car, and she'd been using her father's since arriving in Shalmouth. Unfortunately, the ancient red Ford estate was suffering from recurring carburettor trouble. 'They promised to have the car road-worthy for this evening. I hope they have, otherwise I might be ringing you for another lift!'

Susie frowned. 'You're trying to run the boatyard all day, then sitting by your father's side till the early hours of the morning. Darling, you'll end up in hospital yourself, at this rate! You look shattered already. There are lots of nasty viruses around at the moment, just waiting to strike you when you're down. Don't overdo it, Charlie, will you?'

'No. I'm strong as an ox!' she declared, jutting out her chin in an obstinate mannerism her friend recognised of old. 'You'd be amazed how much I can take before I crumble in defeat!'

The words seemed prophetic the following morning, when Charlotte arrived at the boatyard to face a demoralised-looking Geoff, her father's foreman, and a tearful receptionist.

'It's the roof on the sail-loft, Charlie,' Geoff told her, shaking his head despairingly. 'The wind's ripped half the tiles off. All we need is a heavy shower of rain, and we'll be bailing out!'

'Oh, heavens! It can't be that bad, Geoff, surely?' she exclaimed, eyeing the swollen face of Delia, the young red-haired girl who worked part time answering the telephone and typing whatever letters there were to be typed, and trying to conjecture what could be wrong with her.

'Boyfriend trouble,' Geoff told her darkly, as he followed her up to the sail-loft and watched her horrified examination of the damage. The hole in the roof was at least a foot wide, presenting a framed picture of this morning's fluffy white clouds skimming wildly across a deceptively blue sky.

'I'll get on to the insurance company,' Charlotte said firmly, darting back down to the office and hesitating only slightly before asking Delia to dig out the insurance policies. 'We need to get that hole fixed before it gets any worse. Are there any telephone messages, Delia?'

'Yes—a Mr Smithson rang about a trimaran. He talked to Geoff,' the girl said, rummaging through the filing cabinet.

'I told him we didn't build anything in FRP,' Geoff supplied absently.

'You told him *what*? Geoff, I met him in the Beach Inn a few days ago, and I was hoping he'd ask us to build his boat for him!' She glared at the weather-beaten foreman, whose freckled face was furrowed in disbelief.

'Your father never messed around with reinforced plastics, Charlie. He said wooden hulls were still in demand, and much safer. . .'

'Well, he was quite right, but people wanting racing craft for single-handed transatlantic races aren't primarily looking for *safety*, Geoff!' she exploded, frustration and tiredness making her lose her temper. 'They're looking for *speed*, lightness of handling! They're well aware they could disintegrate at top speed in the middle of the Atlantic ocean, but it's a risk they're prepared to take!'

'All right, all right! There's no need to take that sarcastic tone——'

'Am I interrupting anything?' The deep, laconic voice at the door made Charlie freeze into total immobility. She didn't need to look round. She recognised that voice instantly, even though it was years since she'd seen its owner, and even longer since she'd spoken to him.

'Hello there, Drew.' Geoff greeted him with cautious respect in his voice. 'What can we do for you this morning?'

'How's Jonathan? I just got back from a trip to the Caribbean, and I heard he was in hospital.' Drew's voice had retained its peculiar rasping note, Charlotte registered numbly, battling with the infuriating reaction in her knees as she prepared to turn and face him.

'My father is in a coma,' she heard herself saying, as if from a distance, as she swung slowly round to face him. 'The doctors don't give him much longer to live.'

The words were painful to say, but as her eyes eventually met the pale, narrowed gaze of the man in the doorway, another sort of pain erupted inside her.

'Hello, Charlotte. I heard you were back in Shalmouth.' He spoke without intonation, the curious yellow-amber eyes holding her gaze implacably. A shiver of sensation ran down her spine. He hadn't changed, then. He hadn't mellowed. She recognised that calculating stare, the way he silently weighed things up before passing merciless judgement.

Furious at herself, she felt heat creeping from her chest to the roots of her hair, consumed with a self-consciousness she could have sworn she'd outgrown. Catching a glimpse of herself in the cracked mirror over her father's desk, she registered what an unprepossessing sight she must be. White-faced, with huge smudged shadows under her eyes, in an oversized green sweatshirt belonging to her father, and tight, well-worn denims. Aspects of herself she'd thought she'd grown to live with, mental criticisms of her numerous faults and total lack of desirability to the opposite sex—apparently all it took to bring them flooding back was one long, thoughtful stare from this particular man, she thought bitterly.

'How are you, Drew? I haven't seen you for a long time,' she said politely, reaching furtively behind her for the edge of the desk to prop up her flagging courage.

'I'm fine. How about you? I heard a rumour you were back in Shalmouth for good.'

'That's right. I. . . I'm running Wells Boats,' she said flatly, avoiding Geoff's eyes.

One black eyebrow raised quizzically on Drew's swarthy face.

'Not much left to run, if you ask me,' Geoff muttered bleakly, and she shot a swift, warning glance at him.

'My father had been ill for some time, and things have been getting into a bit of a mess,' she explained shortly, thrusting shaking hands into the pockets of her tight denim jeans, and lifting her chin. 'I believe the boatyard is still quite viable. All it needs is a fresh approach.'

She couldn't take her eyes off Drew as she spoke. In battered oilskin, fisherman's sweater and denims, his short black curls sculpted close to the classic, Roman shape of his head, he looked bigger, darker, more powerful than she remembered him. The shadows of the doorway accentuated the harsh angles and planes of his face, making deep hollows of his eye-sockets. His face spoke volumes about his character. Dark, hard, unapproachable.

He'd said he'd just come back from the Caribbean. Delivering a yacht for someone, she presumed. She'd heard he still did single-handed yacht deliveries himself, even though he'd expanded into other areas now. Shalmouth Skippers wasn't his only source of business any more. There was Shalmouth Sea School, and South West Marinas as well, according to her old sailing club friend Tim Fennel, who now owned his own boatyard further up the river. But she couldn't imagine Drew giving up the dangerous excitement and exhilaration of sailing the oceans alone throughout the roughest months of the year, even if he no longer needed to.

He seemed to thrive on physical hardship. Shalmouth's rough diamond, local hero made good, she thought derisively. Even his presence in the room commanded attention, to the point where all three of them, Geoff, Delia and herself, were standing respectfully before him, as if waiting for some earth-shattering pronouncement. He always appeared supremely confident, casually in control, like a Greek god, as if this kind of reaction was his due. Arrogant devil, she exploded inwardly. Something in her eyes caused an imperceptible hardening of Drew's expression, and for a split second she sensed he was remembering the past. She tensed involuntarily, as if silently preparing for battle.

'*You've* got a fresh approach in mind?' he murmured sardonically, a wealth of chauvinistic mockery hidden beneath the innocent query.

'I've got plenty of ideas,' she snapped briefly, tossing the mane of black curls over her shoulder as she turned away. 'And I've got a lot to do now. Was there anything else?'

There was a long, awkward silence.

'No. Nothing else,' Drew said at last, his deep voice cold. 'I'm sorry about your father. He was a good friend. I'll call in and see him.'

She started to say 'Don't bother,' but stopped herself just in time, appalled at the childish urge to start a slanging match with a man she hadn't met for five years, and who she now realised had never been anything but a stranger.

Her brief encounter with Drew Meredith left a nasty taste in her mouth, but her indignation at his cool mockery gave her the spur she needed to forge ahead with her plans for the yard. Fatigue and anxiety over her father were temporarily banished by this burning need to prove herself worthy of the task she'd been set. By Thursday, she was euphoric. Using every ounce of cunning and public relations expertise she possessed, she managed to retrieve Mr Smithson and convince him that her father's yard was the obvious choice to build his trimaran. Citing their long-established reputation in the town, their superior construction capacity, and pointing out that they could start immediately and give the project their total attention, she extracted a verbal agreement from him and then spent a long, hopeful session with the bank manager, mentally juggling the possibility of employing a naval architect to supervise the project.

Geoff's persistent expression of gloomy foreboding was almost too much to bear, after her successful coup. Anyone would think the wretched man *wanted* to be out of a job, she thought fiercely, when all she was trying to do was to save his livelihood. Geoff had worked for her father for as long as she could remember, and she was very fond of him, and of his second wife Jenny and their two little girls. But he was no motivator. He was a valuable, skilled craftsman, but he'd always been a pessimist. It would be up to her to instil enthusiasm into her small team, and she certainly had no intention of letting Geoff depress her into giving up without a fight. Nor Delia, for that matter. She really needed to have a heart to heart with Delia. The paperwork in the office was a disaster area, and they wasted more time searching for things than they spent on profitable business.

There didn't appear to be a coherent record of anything, she reflected wearily, letting herself into her father's basement flat on Friday night, and collapsing into a chair. She'd spent what felt like a wasted afternoon checking through the labels on the masts jumbled haphazardly in the cellar store-room, trying to find one belonging to a customer who'd rung in the morning and wanted to dispatch his ketch off to Antigua in time for the spring, and she felt almost too tired to move a muscle.

Propelling herself back into action, she scanned the contents of the fridge with a grimace, and made herself a quick, makeshift supper of a cheese roll and a glass of milk. She carried them back into the sitting-room and ate them watching the early evening news, preferring a cross-legged pose on a cushion in front of the gas fire to the hard, uncomfortable sofa.

The small, sea-front flat was serviceable, but it could hardly be called luxurious. There were some tasteful pieces of furniture, mainly antiques from her parents' previous large Regency house on the outskirts of the town. But her father's idea of interior decoration was to strip everything down to essentials, a bit like a tightly run ship. The bare floorboards were varnished an antique pine colour, relieved only occasionally by dark brown rugs, the walls were a stark, utilitarian grey, and the tan-coloured cord sofas were high-backed, and lacking the luxury of extra cushions. Apart from a vast number of books, and stacks of sailing journals, there were hardly any ornaments.

The place was spotlessly clean and meticulously tidy, which she suspected owed more to the devoted 'daily' who scrubbed the place within an inch of its life, twice a week, than to her father's attention to detail. But it lacked a woman's touch, she reflected sadly. She would have added flowered chintz curtains and matching cushions, baskets of dried flowers and pot-pourri, and painted the walls a soft apricot shade to go with the floor.

She washed up, and tidied the small kitchen, then showered to revive herself before her evening at the hospital, shampooing her hair and soaping herself all over under the soothing jets of hot water, finally searching the wardrobe for an alternative to the jeans and sweatshirts she'd lived in since arriving in Shalmouth. Up till now, she hadn't had the time or inclination to bother much with her appearance, but the triumph with Mr Smithson had boosted her morale, given her a small leap of optimism that perhaps things at last were going better, that her father would surely recover, and the boatyard would go from strength to strength.

Most of her smarter outfits were still in her London bedsit, awaiting collection along with her music tapes and pictures and books, but she found a dark green basque-skirt, and added a matching sweater and boots, and a loose, floral jacket. Quickly blow-drying her hair into its usual wild mass of curls, she absently studied her white face and shadowed eyes in the mirror, thinking wryly that if father did surface from his coma he'd have the fright of his life. Worry and lack of sleep had taken their toll. She looked like a ghost! A touch of blusher was called for, and some greeny blue eyeshadow to match her eyes, she decided, hastily pushing her hair back with a couple of emerald combs, and going in search of her make-up. She was just applying the finishing touches when the call came from the hospital.

Her father had taken a turn for the worse, said a calm, dispassionate voice. They advised her to get there as quickly as she could.

Afterwards she couldn't remember a thing about the ten-mile drive to the hospital. The only thing that stuck in her mind was the expression on the ward sister's face, and her numb disbelief that her father had died just minutes before she'd arrived.

She insisted on seeing him. It seemed strangely cathartic to see the peaceful expression on the lean, familiar face, but as she was led out of his room she'd never known such aching emptiness.

She felt suddenly confused, totally disorientated, and very frightened. Stumbling back to the lift, she tried to think coherently about what she should be doing now, vaguely conscious that she had to ring Fiona, that she had to instigate all sorts of complicated funeral arrangements, hardly hearing the sister's voice calling anxiously after her, only half conscious of the tears streaming down her face, blurring her vision. As the lift doors swished open she cannoned blindly into a tall, black-haired man stepping out.

Almost knocked off balance at the force of the collision, the man caught her in his arms, and then tightened his grip around her as she struggled to extricate herself and get past him into the lift, and it was thus that she somehow found herself sobbing uncontrollably on the supple, muscular shoulder of Drew Meredith.

CHAPTER TWO

'DRINK this.' Drew pushed the whisky glass into her hands, then watched her stare at the amber liquid blankly.

'Drink!' he repeated, an unfamiliar note of persuasion in his harsh voice.

Obediently she raised the heavy lead-crystal glass to her lips, and took a gulp. The spirit was fiery and caught the back of her throat. She began to choke, and he took the glass from her and patted her none too gently on the back.

'Go easy with it. Sip it, don't knock it back in one!'

The abrasive command made her jerk her head up defiantly, and she found Drew watching her with a calculating appraisal.

'That's better,' he murmured, his wide mouth twisting slightly. 'There's some colour in your cheeks.'

He hadn't changed at all, she thought bleakly. He still thought fellow human beings were there to be ordered around, controlled. No wonder he was such a loner. Relationships were about give and take. There was no such thing in Drew's embittered vocabulary.

'Will you stop staring at me as if I'm Count

Dracula? This is a house, not a castle on a mountain-top!'

She blinked. 'Sorry,' she said shortly, taking another careful sip of the whisky, and glancing around at the room, with its thick, Elizabethan walls and massive stone fireplace. Drew's house was mellow and welcoming, quite unlike its owner. 'I'd forgotten how bossy you were,' she heard herself adding wryly.

'I didn't bring you back here to trade insults, Charlotte.' His voice was cool, and he turned away from her, strolling across to refill his own glass and taking a quick mouthful immediately afterwards.

'No.' She lowered her eyes from his narrowed stare, annoyed with herself. 'I appreciate your. . .kindness.'

He said an extremely rude word under his breath. 'Your father was an old friend. You were his favourite daughter. What did you expect me to do when you crashed into me in the lift?'

She shrugged. 'Well, you didn't *have* to. . .to take charge of me! Drive me here, telephone Fiona for me, ply me with whisky!'

For the first time, the hard mouth twisted in faint humour. 'Maybe the whisky was a mistake. Hot, sweet tea's the right treatment for shock. Whisky makes people belligerent. But I seemed to remember you had a liking for whisky.'

She took another mouthful, feeling two hot spots of colour beginning to burn on her cheekbones. His casual recollection of one of her personal tastes abruptly resurrected a whole host of other things they'd once known about each other. Silently, she stared at him, grief and exhaustion ridding her of her normal inhibitions. Drew gazed back, and their eyes locked for what seemed an endless moment.

'In moderation,' she said at last, sounding ridiculously prim. Tears welled in her eyes again, and she swallowed convulsively. 'Oh, Drew! I can't bear it— I'm going to miss him so much!'

She fought frantically for control. She'd already ruined Drew's extremely expensive-looking suit, crying all over his shoulder earlier. She was terrified suddenly at the thought of breaking down again, in front of him.

Horrified, she watched him stride across the room, and come down beside her on the velvet chesterfield, pulling her roughly into his arms.

'It's all right. . . I'm OK, really. . .'

'You're not. Cry, Charlotte, don't be afraid to show how much it hurts. . .' The brusque order was muffled against her hair, and she felt his hand move up to press her face hard against his chest. He'd taken off his grey suit jacket, and loosened his tie and the top button of his white shirt. She found her cheek against fine silk, and smooth, laundered poplin, and with a shiver of awareness she allowed herself to relax, just for a second, into the reassuring strength of Drew's arms, while he murmured soothing things to her as if she were a small child.

It seemed ages later that he finally released her,

handing her a clean handkerchief with uncharacteristic chivalry.

'It's a long time since I held you in my arms,' he commented, the casual flatness of his tone belying the intimacy. 'You've lost weight. What have you been doing for the last five years, Charlotte? I caught a glimpse of you when you came home for your mother's funeral last year, but apart from that you've hardly been home, have you?'

'I'm sure you know roughly what I've been doing. Don't tell me Dad never talked about me?'

'You did a fine arts degree at Norwich. You got a job with an auction house in London. I gather from local gossip you've jacked that in. Was that wise?'

'Well, failing a sudden acquisition of superhuman powers, I don't see how I could run Wells Boats *and* do a full-time job in London.'

'True. . .' Something in Drew's expression made her uneasy. She'd been half expecting derision, but the flicker of reaction across the dark face was harder to read. 'Are you sure you know what you're taking on?'

'I know exactly what I'm taking on. My father and my grandfather were boat-builders. Being *female* doesn't render me dead from the neck up. Please don't patronise me, Drew.'

Swallowing the rest of her whisky in an unladylike gulp, she moved fractionally away from him. Glad as she might be of company tonight, sitting here chatting over the last five years with Drew Meredith was about as attractive a prospect as bearding a lion in his den. She felt an urgent need to escape.

'I'd like to go home now, please. . .'

Drew was studying her set face, his own unreadable. The look of cool analysis was painfully familiar, almost as painful as the dull grief inside her. Drew had always had a capacity for total concentration, a facility for pin-pointing all his attention on whatever problem appeared to need solving. Presumably he saw her in terms of a tricky problem, she deduced bleakly, her temper starting to kindle.

'I'll take you to Fiona's,' he said at last, his voice sounding absent, as if he was considering something else entirely.

'I don't want to go to Fiona's tonight!' It was out almost before she thought about what she was saying. When she saw his quizzical expression, she realised she ought to explain, but without being disloyal to Fiona it was difficult to explain that her sister was the last person she wanted to be with tonight. She couldn't face that brisk attitude, the orders to pull herself together. Dad was dead. It might be totally self-indulgent, but she wanted to grieve for him alone, try to come to terms with her loss.

'Then you can stay here. . .'

'No, thanks!' She stood up, her horror clearly showing in her face because Drew's hard mouth twitched mockingly.

'No need to act like a frightened virgin, Charlotte,' he rasped, amused. 'This is a big house.

You met my housekeeper when we arrived. If the
proprieties bother you——'

'It's nothing to do with *proprieties*,' she cut in
stiffly. 'I just want to go back to my father's flat, and
be alone. And just because I happened to bump into
you tonight, it hardly makes you responsible for me!
I've said I'm very grateful for your help so far, but
after all, we're virtually strangers!'

Drew's dark face tightened. 'Strangers?' he
echoed tauntingly. 'That's an interesting description.
Maybe we don't know everything there is to know
about each other, but I'd hardly describe us as
strangers. We spent a month together, that fascinat-
ing *ménage à trois* on board a forty-foot ketch,
remember? You get to know quite a bit about a
person, cooped up on board a yacht!'

'I don't want to talk about that,' she said in a low
voice, the heat in her face nothing to do with the
glow from the whisky. She couldn't believe Drew
would be so callous as to rake things up from the
past. He must have some modicum of sensitivity,
surely?

'I'm just setting the record straight.' He shrugged,
reaching for his glass and taking an aggressive swallow, something in the movement telling her he
wasn't as relaxed and amused as his outward appearance suggested. Drew Meredith wouldn't recognise
a straight record if it hit him in the face, she thought
bitterly.

'I'm surprised you still remember such trivial

things.' She was struggling to keep the tremble out of her voice.

'You nearly drowned one stormy night, as I recall. No doubt I'm cursed with an abnormal memory, but trivial episodes like that tend to stick in my mind.'

'What do you want me to do?' she burst out. 'Go on my knees again, and thank you for saving my life?'

Drew's pale stare was merciless. 'I don't recall you going on your knees,' he said musingly. 'I remember you were so touchingly grateful as we lay naked together in that sleeping-bag, you were eager to thank me in quite a different position!'

She hit out at him without thinking, and her palm made ferocious, ringing contact with his cheek. She was shocked at the tingle in her hand when she dropped her arm.

Horrified, she stared at him. The teasing light in his eyes died away completely, and a livid mark was slowly forming on his face, but he didn't flinch. He didn't move a muscle.

'You've just taught me something new about you,' he murmured finally, his voice laconic. 'Or have you always had a violent streak?'

'Maybe that's something I've developed since we last met!' She was trembling. She'd never hit anyone before in her life. Biting her lip, she realised she still harboured a dark desire to strangle him. 'Are you going to drive me home, or shall I call a taxi?'

'You're not going back to your father's flat on your own tonight,' Drew stated firmly, taking her arm in a grip which brooked no argument and marching her towards the door. 'Stop behaving like a prima donna, and let my housekeeper show you where you can sleep.'

'I really don't want to stay the night here——'

'And I'm really giving you no choice. Maybe we can continue arguing in the morning, but tonight I've had enough.'

The clipped, rasping voice jolted her. How many times had she heard him barking orders in the same unequivocal way? Indignation and anger rose up in her, but suddenly she felt overwhelmed by the traumas of the evening. After the shameful satisfaction of slapping his face, a further showdown with Drew was the last thing she sought tonight.

'I've no nightwear.'

'I'll find you something.' There was an edge to his voice as he summoned his housekeeper and gave instructions, and to her chagrin Charlotte found herself meekly being shown to an elegant guest suite, furnished in restful shades of pink and cream, and politely thanking the kind-faced Mrs Bolton for the thoughtful provision of nightdress and toiletries.

'You're quite sure you don't want any supper?' The housekeeper seemed to be eyeing Charlotte's slender frame as if she foresaw imminent starvation. 'You look very peaky, if you don't mind my saying so. I can cut you a chicken sandwich in no time at all, dear. . .?'

'No, really, thanks. I couldn't eat a thing.'

This was quite true, Charlotte reflected, getting

ready for bed as quickly as she could. She hadn't had much to eat that evening, but her digestive system seemed to have shut down completely. Shock, most likely.

Whose nightdress was she borrowing? she wondered, as she slid into the skimpy wisp of pale pink satin. Surely it couldn't belong to Mrs Bolton? She tried briefly to imagine the matronly, grey-haired housekeeper wearing the garment, without success. A tight little stab of pain pricked her as she realised the likely explanation. Some female friend of Drew's was obviously in the habit of leaving her night attire here, which could have only one meaning. Unless. . .of course, Drew might be married? She hadn't thought of that. It was unlikely, somehow. With his basic dislike and mistrust of women, she found it hard to imagine he'd found a suitable paragon of virtue to meet his impossibly high expectations. . . It was also doubtful if he could have married without her hearing about it on the grapevine, but it was possible. . .anything was possible.

Well, it didn't matter. Drew Meredith's lifestyle held no fascination for her whatsoever.

She was so exhausted, she was sure she'd sleep the instant her head hit the pillow. But sleep stayed tormentingly just beyond her reach. Finally she gave up, getting up to rinse her hot face in the bathroom, and open the sash-window to let in some air. Leaning on the window-sill, she breathed in the salty smell of the estuary, feeling trapped and restless. There was another storm blowing up. The wind was whipping the lacy fronds of a tamarisk hedge below, and scudding black clouds across the moon above the water. What if this gale dislodged the temporary patching on the boatyard roof? She might arrive in the morning to find the entire roof missing. . .Gloomy despondency descended, adding to the dull ache inside over her father's death.

Taking a deep breath, she leaned further out of the window, trying to gauge exactly where she was. Apart from the lights of the villages on the opposite headland, across the estuary, she could see no near neighbours. If the long drive up to it tonight was anything to go by, the old manor appeared to stand alone in considerable grounds, with the wind and rain lashing in from the sea. The river-mouth would act as a wind-break against the worst of the weather. But tonight's storm would be raging merrily across the Channel, whipping the waves into dizzy troughs and towering peaks, like that fateful night on board the ketch with Drew and Colin, on their delivery trip to Menorca.

Closing her eyes, she held her breath, willing the memories of that night to fade into decent obscurity again. But it was no good. Drew's casual taunting had brought it all back. The drama was unfolding itself inexorably in her mind's eye, like a disturbing film, once seen never forgotten. . .

That night had been far wilder than this. The weather in July should have been reasonably predictable, but that summer nothing was predictable. They'd been only half an hour out of Plymouth when a Force Seven had blown up. By the time they reached the north west coast of France the barometer had dropped to one thousand and sixteen millibars and the night the storm broke the wind had been gusting up to Force Nine and even Ten. It hadn't been a good moment for Colin to announce he always got seasick in rough seas.

At the height of the storm, Drew ordered watertight drill to be observed, only himself on deck, Colin and herself below, washboards in place, hatch closed. But she was filled with dread for Drew, as she huddled grimly below trying to hang on to the contents of her stomach. All her long-felt hero-worship for a man ten years her senior, whose self-sufficiency and cool reserve had mesmerised her for years, switched abruptly to a wild anguish for his safety.

She couldn't stay below. It was impossible, sitting there, ducking missiles as the *Menorquina* pitched and rolled, watching Colin's green-tinged face growing more and more fearful, and listening to him mournfully wondering if he was destined to die young, doomed never to know the results of his A levels.

Back on deck, after one incredulous glance at the size of the waves surrounding the ketch, she made sure she was secured by a safety line, and went boldly to Drew's assistance. It was difficult to see much. Apart from the thick blanket of darkness, trails of spume zig-zagged across the water's surface, and the air itself was filled with spray, like a soaking

fog. Talking was hampered by the crash of the sea
and the wind, but in any case Drew was too preoccupied to lash her with his normal scathing sarcasm. Watching the effort it cost his powerful
muscles to swing the *Menorquina*'s bow in line with
each successive, gigantic wave, she had to see his
reasoning for refusing to let her take the helm.

The deck was streaming with water, heaving and
bucking under her rubber boots like a fairground
ride, but she managed to check that Drew had
already disengaged the wind-vane, guessing the
waves were probably coming too thick and fast for
the automatic steering paddle to cope. But the storm
jib, in spite of its toughness, looked to be in danger
of getting damaged under the onslaught of the wind.
Acting on her own instinct, she struggled to the
bows to take it down, and when Drew glanced at her
with a brief nod of approval her heart swelled with
ridiculous pride. She *had* found something she could
help with. She'd managed to be of some use, she
told herself proudly, fighting the elements beside the
man she idolised. Now that she was up here with
Drew, she couldn't imagine anything going wrong.
They would overcome this awesome battle against
the elements together, and he would have new
respect for her. Perhaps he would even come to
treat her as an equal.

Battling with the cumbersome storm jib, as it
billowed awkwardly against her efforts to contain it,
thinking these elated, optimistic thoughts, she was
caught completely off balance when the ketch

lurched violently sideways, dark sky and sea spinning into one stormy black whirl, and she was in the water, beneath the water, choking on huge mouthfuls of salt water, her lungs on fire, nearly bursting with pain, and finding that her whole life, short as it had been, was indeed rushing through her head as she faced the very real prospect of drowning. Colin's morbid premonitions had been right, she found herself thinking dispassionately, the results of her A levels figuring less urgently than the prospect of leaving Drew behind, never knowing what it would be like to really get to know him, to touch and kiss him the way she frankly admitted to herself she wanted to. . .

Retching, gasping for air, she burst to the surface then was dragged under again and again, conscious of the perilous fragility of the safety line which secured her to the ketch in this massively powerful sea. Between snatching air into her lungs whenever she surfaced, she was trying to estimate the incredible weight of her soaked layers of protective foul-weather clothing, plus her own healthily rounded nine stone, which Drew and Colin were grimly trying to haul aboard. They would never manage it, she thought bleakly; water-logged bodies in the water weighed a ton. . . Time was suspended in a continuous nightmare, while the storm raged all around her, and her life dangled on the end of a line.

Later, it seemed a whole lifetime later, she was sprawled on the heaving deck, dimly aware that the peak of the storm seemed to have passed, that the roar of the wind in the rigging held a less threatening note. It had taken both men over fifteen minutes to haul her back on board.

Her knees refused to work. Colin attempted to lift her, and struggled with her sodden weight. Signalling him to take over the wheel, now that the storm was receding, Drew lifted her in his arms and carried her below to the battle-strewn scene in the cabin, with books and kitchen utensils scattered, and floods from the heads, chaos everywhere. He began stripping off her streaming clothes, working with a desperate urgency which held no significance for her at the time. She dimly realised she should have felt embarrassed, but modesty struck her as a minor consideration, a luxury she couldn't afford. She couldn't stop shivering, yet she was almost too numb to shiver. The coldness seemed to be coming from right inside her, creeping insidiously through her. Her body and limbs felt like lead.

'Drew, I'm so cold.' He found a big rough white towel, and tried to chafe sensation back into her frozen body. She hugged the towel around her with numb fingers as he unzipped his own outer clothes and kicked them impatiently aside, catching her as the ketch lurched again and she almost fell. She felt the powerful brace of his legs as he steadied her easily against the motion of the boat. Then, lifting her into his arms again, he carried her into the aft cabin, laying her on the double bunk and unzipping her sleeping-bag.

'Unless you want to die of hypothermia,' he told

her abruptly, 'you'll have to let me get in there with you.'

She was too numb to argue. As casually as if he were stripping alone to take a shower, Drew shed his clothes, and her impressionable gaze was mesmerised on the flat, lean muscles rippling beneath the swarthy gold of his chest, the powerfully wide shoulders and narrow hips. Perhaps out of deference to her youth, he retained a pair of black briefs for the sake of modesty before easing himself into the sleeping-bag beside her, reaching out to zip up the side.

Drew pulled her closely against him and transmitted his raw energy into her chilled body, and, lying passive in his arms, she slept from sheer exhaustion. But when she woke, and felt Drew's unfamiliar body warm and hard against her, she no longer felt passive. The knowledge that she was lying naked in Drew's arms, his powerful maleness moulded intimately against her, had been overwhelming, both mentally and physically. . .

Dragging her wandering thoughts back to the present, Charlotte shivered with cold, wrapping her arms round herself, reflecting wryly that the pink nightdress was totally unsuitable for standing by open windows on cold February nights.

Drew might have saved her from hypothermia in the stormy darkness of the Atlantic ocean five years ago, but if she wasn't careful she'd succumb to the same fate in the relative safety of this bedroom.

She retreated to the warmth of her bed and pulled

the duvet around her thankfully, determinedly fending off the unwelcome memories continuing to creep into her mind. The past ought to stay where it belonged—firmly in the past. She was crazy to rake up those silly, naïve mistakes. The tensions during that voyage had been numerous and complex. Drew, herself, and Colin. . . It struck her as hopelessly sordid now, five years on.

Tiredness came to the rescue, at last, blotting out thoughts of Drew Meredith, and even her sadness over her father, and she fell asleep almost before she'd had time to wriggle a comfortable place for her head on the pillow.

The creakings and groanings of an antiquated plumbing system woke her early. She lay in the warm, secure cocoon of duck-down quilt, listening sleepily to the sounds around her. The muted rattles and clanks from the pipes made her think of her parents' old house, with its wide mahogany banisters curving down endless flights of stairs, and which to her mother's horror she'd frequently slid down.

Drew's house was much older, though, at least sixteenth century, with its ancient leaded-light windows, thick stone walls and uneven floors. Turning her head slowly to the side, she could see pale winter sunshine streaming into the bedroom through a chink in the heavy cream brocade curtains. The storm had obviously blown itself out. She could hear wood pigeons cooing in the trees outside. There was a peaceful stillness about the old house.

The joy to be awake and alive on such a day

vanished abruptly, when sleep finally receded and memory returned. Her father was dead. The pain was like a blow to her stomach, rising to her throat, and she turned over in bed to cradle the pillow against her, swallowing back the tears. Life suddenly seemed a bleak, grey landscape stretching ahead of her. It took all her reserves of will-power to lever herself out of bed, into a hot shower, and then make her way down through the labyrinth of passages to the kitchen.

Finding the kitchen wasn't as difficult as she'd expected. A savoury waft of frying bacon led her straight there, and she paused on the threshold, surprised to see Drew, not Mrs Bolton, presiding over a vast Aga.

She hesitated, unable to drag her eyes away from the sight of him, casually dressed in denims and check shirt, a butcher-stripe apron round his neck, the two lean black Labradors she'd glimpsed last night sprawled as close to his feet as possible. The dogs had spotted her, and began scrambling up to welcome her with cautious wags of the tail.

'Good morning. How did you sleep?' Drew glanced at her briefly as he spoke, his expression bland.

'Fine, thanks.'

'Do you want an egg?'

'No, thanks. Just toast and tea, please.'

'Don't tell me you can't eat bacon, tomato and fried bread? This used to be one of your favourites!'

'True. . .' Why did the wretched man have to

display his remarkable memory for detail? she wondered savagely. 'But I don't feel like eating much this morning.'

'You've got a busy spell ahead of you,' Drew said grimly, steering her to a chair at the large scrubbed pine table, and laying a knife and fork deliberately in front of her. 'So if you want me to drive you back into Shalmouth to face it all, you eat a decent breakfast.'

Before she could protest, he'd placed a glass of orange juice and a plate of crisply fried breakfast before her, and joined her at the table to calmly tackle his own portion. Short of sitting defiantly, staring at the food, which would seem a touch childish, she had no option but to eat. And, after the first couple of mouthfuls, she found her appetite returning, and finished it all.

'That's better,' Drew murmured, eyeing her clean plate with a twist of a smile. 'You used to be a lot rounder, Charlotte. I don't think I like you anorexic.'

'I don't recall you liking me much when I was rounder!' she snapped before she could prudently refrain from comment. Drew's answering glance brought colour into her cheeks.

There was a short, charged silence, then Drew stood up and cleared away their plates, moving behind her with familiar economy of energy. She heard the toaster click down, and the kettle switch on, and realised she was gripping her hands together under the table, a sure-fire way of giving herself indigestion. Relax, she told herself silently. Letting out her breath in a long sigh, she closed her eyes. The ordeal was nearly over. Once she was back in Shalmouth, she could try her hardest to avoid him whenever possible.

'Tea and toast. With Marmite, not marmalade. Right?'

She abruptly opened her eyes as Drew returned, and forced a polite smile. 'Thanks. I'm not sure why you're waiting on me like this.'

'Normally Mrs Bolton would do it,' Drew admitted, spinning a chair round and straddling it, his arms resting on the back, a black coffee in front of him. 'But she goes into Exeter early on Saturday mornings. Beats the rush at the hypermarket.'

'Oh. I see.'

'How are you feeling now, Charlotte?' His voice deepened, and she tensed automatically. Drew's ruthless derision, his casual mockery, she could take. These odd flashes of kindness were unnerving her completely. They were triggered by pity, of course. Drew had caught her at a vulnerable moment last night, seen her in a state of semi-collapse, all the raw emotion on display. She decided she could bear anything, the pain of her father's death, the loneliness and despair deep inside her, anything but this insidious pity from Drew Meredith.

'I'm fine,' she said abruptly, avoiding the piercing yellow gaze and spreading Marmite thickly on her toast.

'You were pretty shaken up last night. Losing

your father so soon after your mother dying can't be easy. You're very young to cope with that, and the boatyard business.'

'I'm twenty-three, Drew,' she said evenly, cutting the toast into triangles and taking a small bite from one corner. 'I've lived away from home for five years. I assure you I'm a vastly different person——'

'From the inexperienced little seventeen-year-old I took on as crew that summer?' Drew took up where she'd abruptly left off.

'Let's not rake all that up again.' She took a sip of tea, proud of her composure as she lifted the cup to her lips.

'All right, we'll leave the past alone, for now,' Drew agreed calmly, drinking some of his coffee. 'Let's concentrate on the present. When all the dust has settled, what do you intend to do with the boatyard? Presumably you and Fiona will inherit?'

'I presume so. . . I can't know the details until my father's will is read, of course. I'll ring the solicitor when I get back to Shalmouth.'

'Where do you anticipate living? In your father's flat?'

She shrugged. 'Who knows? No doubt that will go to both Fiona and myself as well. She may want her half-share straight away, in which case I'll have to find somewhere else.'

She stared at him coldly, challenging him to probe any further, and he made a wry face.

'You think it's none of my business,' he observed flatly.

'For the life of me, I can't see how anything I decide *could* be your business.'

'Like it or not, Charlotte, your father was a close friend of mine. I was extremely fond of him,' Drew said expressionlessly. 'And you and I have links from the past. Admit it.'

She grated her chair back violently.

'Oh, I admit it, Drew! There was a time when I was short-sighted enough to put you on a pedestal! You were everything I ever dreamed of being—a yacht master ocean, taking off on your own for months on end, single-handedly delivering yachts around the world. There was nothing I wanted more than to sail across oceans and navigate by the stars and the sun! You had all the freedom that goes with being male!'

Drew had stood up as well, his eyes glitteringly amused beneath half-closed lids.

'There's nothing to stop females being as adventurous as males, if they want it badly enough. But I can recall something you wanted, Charlotte,' he said softly, tauntingly, 'and it had nothing to do with dreaming of being a boy!'

She blinked at the dazzling mockery in his eyes, forcing herself to smile calmly.

'We all make stupid mistakes when we're younger. . .not everyone stores them up and flings them back in our face when we'd prefer to forget all about them!' Her heart was pounding deep in her chest, and she wrenched her eyes from his. 'Do you mind if I get back into Shalmouth now? As you said, I'll have a lot to do today.'

'I don't mind at all,' Drew said bleakly, standing aside to let her sweep in what she hoped was a dignified manner out of the kitchen. 'Breakfast is the wrong time for this kind of conversation.'

'Is there a right time?'

'Without a doubt, Charlotte.' He followed her into the hall and watched her run lightly upstairs to fetch her possessions. There was that odd, cold inflexion in his voice again, she thought warily, quickly straightening the room and collecting her bag and jacket. She couldn't identify it, but it certainly didn't indicate any desire for friendship or reconciliation.

Which was just as well, she added to herself, as she returned to the hall to find him waiting by the window, his back to her, tall and motionless, the aura of loose-limbed power he exuded striking a warning shiver through her. If there was one complication above all others she could well live without, it was the thought of facing another lethal emotional entanglement with a man like Drew Meredith.

CHAPTER THREE

'AT LEAST now the ordeal of the funeral is over,' Jocelyn Adams said kindly, 'life can begin to get back to normal.'

Charlotte managed a thin smile at her father's old friend, across the wide, leather-topped desk, and Jocelyn's faded blue eyes smiled back.

'Yes. I'm sure you're right. It's just that I'm not quite sure what "normal" is any more!' She laughed shortly. 'I know this sounds horribly prosaic, but having given up my job in London and come back to run the boatyard, I need to know where I stand, financially. I've no savings of any kind. My salary in London was fairly low. And with the bombshell over the boatyard insurance, and needing a new roof. . .'

Jocelyn's florid face puckered into a deep frown. 'Bombshell over the insurance?' he repeated tentatively.

'Dad neglected to update the premiums.'

'The yard's not insured?' Jocelyn was incredulous.

'Partly. It's grossly under-insured. Delia and Geoff dug out the premiums the other day. . .' Charlotte trailed off with a sigh, recalling the dire discovery with fresh horror. 'I feel as if the rug has been pulled from under me. How do you think the bank manager will react when he finds out the money he's advancing on the trimaran could be needed for repairs to the premises instead?'

'Oh, dear me! Dear me, how dreadful! Yes. . . I'm afraid your father let the paperwork side slip a little. He'd been unwell for a long time, and his illness accelerated after your mother died.'

'Yes. I know that now. Unfortunately he managed to hide his illness from me until he fell and hit his head. . . I suppose really it was my fault for not coming home more often. . .' She bit her lip, avoiding Jocelyn's eyes.

'Don't blame yourself, my dear. I knew Jonathan since we were boys together. He was far too proud to let you know he was ill. Elizabeth's death hit him very hard, you know. He'd always hoped they could get back together. . .' The solicitor steepled his fingers, with a sad shake of his white head.

'Dad didn't want the divorce?'

'No. Jonathan had his faults, he'd freely admit them, but he strongly believed in marriage, family responsibilities.'

'Did he ever. . .?' her voice tailed away, and she tried again, 'Jocelyn, did my father ever tell you why he and my mother split up?'

'My dear child——'

'It's just that they argued a lot over me. Mum wanted me to be like Fiona, pretty dresses, ribbons. . . Dad loved me being a tomboy, but he wanted to please Mum as well. The result was. . .rather fraught!'

'You never knew quite who to please?' Jocelyn

summed up gently, his wise blue eyes full of understanding. 'My dear, your parents' divorce had nothing to do with you. There was another man involved. . .'

Charlotte was stunned. 'Another *man*?' It took quite an acrobatic imagination to visualise her mother having an affair, even though she'd been much younger than Dad. She'd always been so. . .prim, pious. 'Who was it, for heaven's sake?'

Jocelyn's expression was all professional blandness. 'The man is dead. . .naming him would achieve nothing, Charlotte. I only told you to stop you feeling guilty about things that are out of your control, my dear.'

He stood up and came round the desk, and she stood up too, giving him an impulsive hug. Dear Jocelyn, he'd been a family friend for years. He had the sort of comforting wisdom which encouraged confidences.

'Does there have to be all this cloak and dagger stuff about reading Dad's will, Jocelyn?' she complained lightly. 'Couldn't you just tell me now?'

'Beth's very keen to cook you and Fiona what she calls a "good square meal" tonight, in any case,' Jocelyn said calmly. 'And I'd rather get everyone together. It's easier that way.'

She gazed at him doubtfully, but it was obvious she would get nothing further from him for the time being.

'Jocelyn's behaving like a character out of an Agatha Christie film!' Fiona accused later, as Beth ushered them into deep chintz armchairs either side of a blazing log fire and plied them with dry sherry and canapés. 'Dad's will can't be *that* complicated! What's all the mystery about?'

Beth's perceptive brown eyes glanced shrewdly at Jocelyn and she calmly excused herself to check on the meal. Charlotte looked at Fiona, a sudden knot of apprehension in the pit of her stomach. While she wished Fiona weren't in such an aggressive mood, it was unlike Jocelyn to stage such a theatrical scenario.

'Yes, now we *are* all together, could we read Father's will right now, please? I honestly don't think I can stand this tension any longer!' Charlotte smoothed the soft black velvet of her evening trousers, and fixed a pleading gaze on Jocelyn.

'Yes, of course, but. . .' Jocelyn cleared his throat, and walked across to the window, peering between the curtains. Charlotte and Fiona exchanged incredulous looks. 'I'm sorry, but there is another party involved,' he explained heavily, returning to sit down. 'I was rather anxious to wait until he arrived——'

'Another *party*?' Charlotte's brain was racing, suddenly. What on earth could her father have done? Who in the world could be a joint beneficiary? Apart from herself and Fiona, there was no one. . .

'Jocelyn, I am about to scream!' Fiona said brusquely. '*Who* is the other "party"?'

'The son of a very old friend of your father's, Guy Benedict.'

'Guy Benedict never had a son!' asserted Fiona. 'Guy and Mary Benedict never had any children!'

'Andrew is Guy Benedict's illegitimate son.' Jocelyn sighed. 'Your father and Guy Benedict were at Harrow together, served in the Navy together in the war, and remained close friends for a long time. You probably knew that your father's first wife was Mary Benedict's sister?'

They both nodded, mystified. This was so much old history, facts known but stored away as unimportant.

'Many years ago, Guy helped your father financially with the boatyard. It was facing bankruptcy when a customer reneged on an order just before completion. He became a sleeping partner——'

'I knew that!' Charlotte interrupted, frowning. 'But Guy Benedict and Father fell out years ago. Years before I was even born!'

'That was because of Andrew,' Jocelyn pointed out evenly. 'Guy Benedict was a bit of a "ladies' man". There was always friction between Guy and Jonathan over that. I suppose Jonathan felt angry on Mary's behalf. Anyway, thirty-odd years ago Guy had a brief fling with a young Greek-Cypriot woman, who helped nurse his wife when she was ill. Andrew was the result.'

Jocelyn got up and went to stand with his back to the fire.

'Your father never forgave Guy for the casual way

he treated the whole thing. Deceiving Mary, letting the baby be handed over to the social services for adoption——'

'Very noble and touching, but I don't see what this has to do with Dad's will!' Fiona cut in acidly, sipping her sherry and glaring hard at Jocelyn.

'Presumably Dad has left a share of the boatyard to this Andrew?' Charlotte's voice didn't sound quite like her own. She swallowed hard.

'Precisely. Andrew inherits forty per cent. You and Fiona have thirty per cent each.'

'I see. . .'

'That's thirty per cent too much for me, unless there's any money in it. I know absolutely nothing about running a boatyard——'

'Fee!' Charlotte turned horrified eyes on her sister, but the blue gaze was unrepentant.

'It's true. The sooner we sell, the better!'

Jocelyn intervened. 'I've taken the liberty of informing Andrew of the terms of the will. I've invited him here tonight so that you can meet him, talk things over. . . Forgive me for jumping the gun, letting him know before you did. But I wanted to break the news of his inheritance to him diplomatically. I wasn't sure how much he knew about his parentage. It might have been rather unfair to spring that on him tonight, for the first time.'

'I can't understand why Dad didn't tell me about this!' Charlotte was hardly listening to Jocelyn's rather pedantic explanations; she was busy trying to marshal her confused reactions.

'I'm sure he intended to, my dear.'

She suddenly remembered the night her father had been trying to tell her something, before he'd drifted off into the coma he'd never come out of. Jocelyn was right, this must have been the important thing he had been trying to explain to her. Dad had tried to tell her, but he'd slipped away before he'd got round to it. She raked an unsteady hand through her dark curls, her brain racing. Why had he done it? To repay a debt of honour, maybe? Or to compensate for the son he'd never had? The latter brought an unpleasant heaviness to her heart.

'Maybe we could buy this person out?' she suggested cautiously.

'That may prove difficult.' Jocelyn fetched a thick document from his desk. 'Your father borrowed against the flat in St Michael's Crescent, as well as on the family house your mother lived in after their divorce. The upshot, I'm afraid, is that the flat is already spoken for, by the finance company——'

'Sounds familiar!' Fiona was bitter, and Charlotte knew she was referring to the situation after their mother had died, when the house had been found to be in a similar situation. 'Father spent his whole life pouring money down the drain on that boat business. Mum told me she just couldn't take any more of it!'

Charlotte ignored her sister's outburst, sick inside with misery and apprehension. Poor Dad. He'd never confided these worries—he must have been weighed down with all this for years. No wonder he'd been ill. If only he hadn't rejected Guy Benedict's largess on a point of morality. Guy had been a financial wizard, revered in the City. Whatever his dubious personal morals, he was exactly the partner her father had needed. Dad had been a wonderful craftsman, but hopeless with figures.

'You obviously talked to Dad about this.' She turned level eyes on Jocelyn. 'Did he explain his reasons to you?'

The solicitor raised his shoulders slightly, in a weary gesture. 'Jonathan felt very strongly about the way the boy was treated. He wanted to make a gesture of recognition. I think he wanted to make up to him somehow, for having a thoroughly rotten father.'

'Typical,' murmured Fiona, draining her sherry. 'Always the romantic idealist!'

'Stop it!' Charlotte couldn't take any more of Fiona's sniping, rounding on her angrily. 'Mother may have coloured your opinion, but Dad loved you very much. Try to take a more balanced view, Fee, for heaven's sake!'

'And perhaps your father did have a realistic motive, as well?' Jocelyn pointed out quietly. 'He may have had reason to believe a third shareholder would have capital to invest?'

Fiona was about to retaliate when Beth made a timely return, wiping her hands on her apron with an air of triumph.

'Right, come quickly. I've nursed this asparagus soufflé to a crucial stage, and it needs eating pronto!

Andrew will just have to take his chances when he arrives!'

Charlotte was lost in thought as they were ushered into the dining-room. Firelight flickered on shining glass and silverware, on the oval table, and the aroma of Beth's famous steak and kidney pie was wafting gently from the kitchen beyond. She'd always loved Beth and Jocelyn's old Devon long-house, with its homely, haphazard jumble of furnishings and colours. This style reflected her own eclectic tastes far more comfortably than the austere style favoured by her mother. She would like her own home to look rather like this, one day. Complete with a cat like Magnus, the huge blue Persian stretched luxuriously before the fire.

She stared into the flames, turning over Jocelyn's surprise revelations in her mind. It came as a shock to learn she only had a thirty-per-cent share in the yard. Even with all the problems besetting her at present, the thought of having to defer to another person over policy decisions wasn't a prospect she relished. Fiona, by rights, should prove an ally, but her sister was a law unto herself. Together they would wield the larger proportion of power, but there was no guarantee that she and Fiona would agree on anything. That left this newcomer with a disturbing amount of leverage. . .

There was a knock at the front door, and Jocelyn left the bottle of wine he was opening and went to answer it. There was a low murmur of voices in the hall. Charlotte glanced at Fiona, who raised eloquent eyebrows. The door opened, and Jocelyn ushered a very tall, dark-skinned man into the dining-room. In the dim light just inside the door, there was a glimpse of gypsy-black hair, just brushing a very white collar, and an impression of well-honed athletic muscle beneath the expensive cut of a dark suit.

Charlotte raised her chin, hackles already up, preparing to assess this interloper and analyse his potential nuisance value. Then she saw his face, and the militant mood vanished in a rush of shock. She went hot all over, then icy cold.

'Here he is at last!' Jocelyn was saying evenly, apparently oblivious of the sudden build-up of tension which seemed to Charlotte to be causing the whole room to vibrate. 'Andrew, let me introduce you to Charlotte and Fiona Wells. Girls, this is Andrew Benedict. . .though it occurs to me you might already know him, of course, as Andrew Meredith, owner of Shalmouth Sea School?'

'You're very quiet, Charlotte?' Drew was accepting a glass of cognac from Jocelyn at the end of an excellent meal she'd hardly tasted, and was leaning back in his chair with a mellow cloud of Havana cigar smoke drifting around him. 'Do I take it you haven't much to say about our new business partnership?'

'You knew, didn't you?' she said woodenly, flicking her eyes over him with cool resentment. Drew's gaze narrowed assessingly as he stared back.

'Not positively. Jonathan mentioned it in the past. In some ways I hoped he'd forget all about it.' The lazy stare was moving thoughtfully over her slender figure, lingering on the swell of her breasts beneath the white silk wrap-over blouse, and she felt her cheeks grow hotter with indignation.

'Oh, did you? In that case, you won't mind selling your share to me!'

'And what do you propose to buy my share with? Monopoly money?' The deep voice was softly taunting.

'I'll go to the bank! Get a loan. . .'

'Another one? That's in addition to settling outstanding debts, funding this ambitious project with Greg Smithson, and paying for the new roof, I presume?'

Charlotte discovered she was so angry her hands were shaking. In fact she was shaking all over. Thrusting her fists into the soft pockets of her green velvet jacket, she lifted her chin defiantly and glared into the mocking amber eyes.

'So you've been *snooping* around, already?' she accused in a furious undertone. 'Who gave you all that information? Geoff or Delia?'

The mocking light in the half-lidded gaze grew stronger, fuelling her temper even more.

'It's hardly fair to shop my "mole",' he replied thoughtfully, 'but if it saves the poor girl from the thumbscrews and the rack tomorrow, I'd better confess it was Delia.'

'I can't believe even *you* would stoop to pumping a young typist for confidential information!'

'Perhaps "pump" is too strong a word?'

Charlotte glared at him. His smugly superior attitude was unbearably provocative.

'Don't tell me—you're the "boyfriend trouble" Geoff was warning me about? You've been taking Delia out?'

The disbelief in her voice made him laugh. '"Taking her out" is wide of the mark, as well. Stop looking so prim and disapproving, Charlotte! Let's put it diplomatically—Delia has a habit of dogging my footsteps.'

A wave of understanding was followed by a sick feeling in her stomach. Delia had a crush on Drew? The parallels with her own past behaviour were too close for comfort.

'I see. So you string the poor girl along and make use of her devotion whenever it suits you!'

'I don't make use of her in any way.' Drew wasn't smiling any more. 'Delia knows where she stands. She just has a problem coming to terms with it.'

Charlotte glared at him ferociously, and he leaned slightly backwards, the glitter of amusement returning.

'You're not going to hit me again, I hope?' he enquired blandly. 'You really will have to learn to swallow that pride of yours, Charlotte. As for the boatyard, you've got a lot of enthusiasm, but you'll need to bow to my superior knowledge on certain matters!'

Drew was deliberately goading her, and she was contemplating something far more homicidal than merely hitting him. Gritting her teeth, she said as evenly as she could, 'Precisely how do you arrive at this "superior knowledge"? Unless you think being male gives you an instant head-start? In that case, you're wrong! You've sailed around the world a lot, but you're not a boat-builder. My grandfather started Wells Boats. And my father taught me everything he knew. He was a brilliant craftsman——'

'I'm a naval architect,' Drew interrupted flatly, exhaling a spiral of fragrant smoke and eyeing her thoughtfully.

She did her best to disguise the jolt of surprise his announcement gave her. Drew's background had always remained shadowy, with no mention ever made of his life before he had arrived in Shalmouth. This unexpected piece of information emphasised the vast area of Drew's life she knew nothing about.

'You look surprised. You didn't know that?'

'How should I have known?' she queried derisively, impatient with the persistent flicker of curiosity inside her. 'I'll admit I used to be intrigued by your air of mystery, but you weren't in the habit of giving away much information about yourself!'

He shrugged slightly, a mocking twist on his lips. '*Mea culpa*. But you were just a kid—how was I to know you were burning with curiosity about my personal background?'

'Meaning you weren't inclined to talk to a stupid

little school-leaver with a giant crush on you?' She forced a light laugh. 'Quite understandable. Well, I may still be ten years younger than you, but I'm not just a kid any longer. And besides, it wasn't just me you were secretive with. Dad used to bring home the latest rumours about you from the bar at the Beach Inn. You should have heard the improbable stories circulating about you when you first came to Shalmouth!'

She was sufficiently furious with him to enjoy the flicker of discomfort across his normally implacable face.

'Maybe I should hear them now?' he probed lightly, a touch of steel beneath the surface.

'Don't look so worried! I don't think anyone really believed you were an escaped prisoner, or an undercover member of the Special Boat Service, or a closet terrorist awaiting orders!'

Drew threw back his head and laughed out loud, drawing interested glances from Beth and Fiona.

'Did you believe any of it?'

'Well, I was only about fifteen,' she confessed, her own lips twitching at his infectious amusement. 'In the absence of solid facts, they all sounded glamorous possibilities!'

'Well, to avoid further wild speculation, maybe I'd better come clean about my "mysterious" past right now,' he said, sobering as he subjected her to a long, sardonic scrutiny. 'Feel free to interrogate me at length.'

He was still mocking her, she realised, shrinking

from showing an overt interest in his personal background. But curiosity overcame pride.

'I admit I'm baffled by your connection with my father. How come I didn't know anything about it?'

He shrugged slightly. 'Maybe your father didn't think you'd be interested. How close were you?'

'My father and I were very close,' she said stiffly. 'He often confided in me. . .we used to talk everything over together. . .' Even as she spoke, she realised this was more wishful thinking than reality—a fact Drew swiftly seized on.

'Maybe he only told you what he thought you'd like to hear?' he suggested, his face deadpan. 'Did he ever tell you about the problems with the boatyard? Did he tell you he was ill?'

'No. . .' She'd forgotten how ruthless Drew could be.

'Perhaps he didn't want to upset you, or worry you.' Was there a hint of pity in his deep voice? It was hard to tell, but if there was it was the last thing she wanted.

'Maybe you're right,' she said coolly, dismissing his probing. 'Let's get back to your connection with my father. How did he know you were Guy Benedict's son, in the first place? Did he keep tabs on you all through your childhood?'

'No. I came to Shalmouth to trace my real father. Your father heard about it, and introduced himself. My meeting with Guy Benedict wasn't a big success,' the flat voice betrayed no emotion, 'but at least I found out what happened to my real mother.'

Drew paused fractionally, and she waited. The dark features were shuttered, and she was dimly conscious of a pain inside him being coldly denied an outlet.

'Apparently her husband beat her up once too often, and he was jailed for her manslaughter.' He grimaced at her shocked reaction. 'Sordid, isn't it?'

For the first time, she felt a stab of pity for Drew Meredith. She caught herself up sharply. Why waste pity on a man like Drew? She couldn't afford to let her guard slip enough to show compassion.

'No more sordid than half the stories in the tabloids, I suppose,' she murmured. 'And at least I know now where you get your dark skin from—your mother was Greek-Cypriot, Jocelyn said?'

'That's right. Interesting combination, wasn't it? Half English upper-middle class, half foreign immigrant from a family of ten.'

The ruthless self-mockery was painful to listen to. She looked down at her clasped hands in her lap, carefully inspecting the pale half-moons of her short, clear-varnished nails.

'What were your adoptive parents like?'

'Nice people.' He sounded genuinely affectionate for a moment. 'Bill and Grace Meredith. They live on the west coast of Scotland. Bill ran a small sailing school, mostly dinghies. Grace was heavily into social work. They're both retired now. I visit when I can. But I left home at seventeen, so I've lost touch with them to a large extent.'

'So you left to go to university?'

'Not straight away. I joined the Navy.' Drew smiled thinly. 'I was in it for five years. Two years of it spent on nuclear submarines. Incidentally, that's supposed to be a good character reference. The conditions down there for two months at a stretch are a trifle cramped, so they test for psychological flaws.' His eyes glittered with cold amusement. 'I'm guaranteed not to run amok with a knife under stress!'

'Well, that's a comforting thought. Unless they were particularly short of recruits that year?'

She sipped her coffee, her dark green eyes veiled by her lashes as she avoided his gaze.

'If we're going to trade insults again,' Drew murmured sardonically, 'we'd better confine our discussions to business.'

His casual glance round the room made her aware for the first time how closely their low-voiced conversation was being observed by the others in the party, particularly Fiona.

'Tonight doesn't strike me as a particularly good occasion for a business discussion,' she countered frostily, watching as he leaned back in his chair, his long eyes narrowing ominously.

'No? Surely it's an ideal opportunity to air some of those "fresh approaches" you were talking about?' he prompted smoothly, his gaze lidded.

'I'm sure you already know everything there is to know from your cynical use of poor Delia!'

The cool gaze darkened. 'All right. If you're not prepared to discuss your proposals with me tonight, let's convene a meeting first thing tomorrow morning.' He took a swig of his brandy, his eyes suddenly gleaming as hard and cold as platinum. 'As I'm the largest single shareholder, I suggest you and Fiona come to my office at the sea school. I'll get my secretary to draw up a rough agenda. The first thing we need to talk about is pulling down that crumbling old building, and turning the site into a new marina and sailing school.'

He leaned forward to stub out his cigar purposefully in the ashtray, coldly amused as he watched her jaw drop in disbelief.

'I'd like you to give that proposal some thought before tomorrow's meeting.'

CHAPTER FOUR

TO DESCRIBE Drew's office as plush would definitely be an understatement, Charlotte reflected, as she shifted resentfully on her seat and watched the svelte blonde secretary pouring coffee at a side-table. She felt like a defiant adolescent summoned before the headmaster, she realised, and fought hard to rid herself of the feeling. The trouble was, old habits died hard. Years of looking up to Drew, respecting his sharp intellect and his enviable knowledge of the sea and sailing, had left their mark on her. She was in bitter conflict with him, yet she still felt strangely in awe of him.

Snap out of it, she scolded herself silently. He's just another man, fallible and human like the rest of them. And conceited and egotistical into the bargain. And this office was definitely 'delusions of grandeur', she told herself, silently mocking to ease her taut emotions. It didn't even seem to match its owner. The fitted mahogany furniture, dark blue velvet-pile carpet, sophisticated array of electronic equipment on the desk, struck an oddly incongruous note against Drew's wind-tousled black curls, well-worn denims and thick navy guernsey. But then he was an unpredictable character, she reminded herself. If there was one thing that could be relied on about Drew Meredith, it was that he would balk at conforming to an accepted pattern. If he chose to operate from a luxurious office suite, he would dress like one of his hired boat skippers to fool everyone. He was just bloody-minded by nature.

'You're not facing reality, Charlotte,' Drew was saying calmly. 'The boatyard is virtually bankrupt, the premises are falling to pieces, the insurance won't cover the repairs, and you've no personal security to obtain another bank loan. You haven't even got anywhere to live, as of next weekend!'

'Facing reality never was her strong point,' Fiona murmured, unforgivably, accepting coffee from the secretary and crossing her legs to reveal the shapely, slightly dimpled knees Charlotte had always rather envied. 'She lives in a dream-world, just like Dad used to!'

Charlotte examined her own denim-clad legs, stretched out in front of her, thanking the cool-faced blonde for her black coffee. She switched her gaze broodingly from Drew, to her sister, and back again, picking up familiar signals from Fiona with a sinking heart. Her sister found Drew attractive. She could detect it in every movement and glance. Salt on the wound, she reflected bitterly. Searching Drew's harsh mask for signs of reciprocation was a waste of time, of course. Drew was adept at hiding his feelings. At the moment she would get more information from a blank computer screen.

Abruptly standing up, she took her coffee over to the window behind Drew's huge mahogany desk, eyeing the view while she struggled with her emotions. A criss-cross expanse of wooden pontoons, with serried ranks of moored yachts, stretched almost as far as the eye could see on this protected part of the river estuary.

'Where I intend to live is my affair,' she said at last. 'I'm quite capable of looking after myself. What I want to know is why you're suggesting knocking down Wells Boats to make room for another marina. For pity's sake, Shalmouth is bursting with marinas. . . Look at this lot out here!'

Drew had stood up too, and joined her at the window, over six feet of laconic strength topping her own respectable height by several inches. His nearness affected her more than she cared to show, and she resisted the urge to shrink away as he stood close beside her.

'Extra marina space for Shalmouth Sea School would make sure my company keeps its competitive edge. There are plenty of smaller sailing schools in competition now.' The deep voice was flat, uncompromising.

'You expect *me* to care whether your company stays top dog?' she questioned witheringly.

'But we'd be shareholders, too!' Fiona snapped impatiently. 'And there's far more money in the leisure side. To be honest, I think I agree with Drew. His suggestion sounds far more practical than trying to get an antiquated business like Wells Boats back on a profitable basis!'

'So that's all that matters, is it?' Charlotte's

breasts rose jerkily as she fought for control, sea-green eyes flashing as she glanced from Fiona to Drew. 'Profit? Never mind family loyalty? Never mind my father's *misplaced* affection for someone he felt had a raw deal from his own father?'

She put her cup down on Drew's desk with a clatter, thrusting a trembling hand through her dark curls. She felt sick with anger. Glancing stormily from Fiona's cool indifference to Drew's dark detachment, she realised that bursting into tears and lashing out wildly would get her nowhere. She had to try to negotiate, to reason this out.

'I accept that profit is important,' she began again, desperately hanging on to her temper, 'but I happen to think I *can* make Wells Boats show a profit. If we build Greg Smithson's trimaran, and it wins its class in the transatlantic, the spin-off publicity will be all we need. Plus, the premises have room for plenty of dinghy building. We can build at least four, if not five dinghies a year, and revive the sail-making side, and the chandlery. All it needs is some initial investment——' She heard her voice take on a pleading note, and stopped abruptly, furious with herself. Why should she have to *plead* with her sister, and Drew Meredith?

'Initial investment?' Drew's tone was clipped, unmoved. 'It would take hefty capital outlay to get Wells Boats back in business, and those old premises don't justify the cost. As for Greg Smithson's trimaran, Wells have no experience of building that type of craft——'

'It'll be a new challenge!'

'Or an expensive mistake.'

'So what happens to all my father's employees? They're just thrown out of a job, is that the plan?' She found she was so furious her throat was tight with pent-up emotion.

'We're hardly talking vast numbers. Six at most, I suspect some of those on a part-time basis.'

'We're still talking about *people*! Not figures on a balance sheet!'

'Simmer down, Charlie. . .' Her sister's tone was bored as she stood up, smoothing down her smart lovat-blue business suit, softened at the neck by a very feminine frill of white lace. 'I've got to dash, I'm afraid.' She smiled apologetically at Drew, collecting her Filofax from the desk. 'I've got to meet an important client for lunch. I'll let you two thrash this out between you—after all, you both know a lot more about boats than I do! But, Charlie, can't you see you're making exactly the same mistakes Dad always made when it came to business? Letting sentiment rule your judgement?'

On this parting shot, Fiona sauntered out of the office, with a brief flutter of her fingers as she disappeared.

There was a long, charged silence after she'd gone. Drew had rocked himself back in his chair, physically relaxed, yet somehow managing to exude an aura of watchful awareness. Charlotte felt as if her chaotic emotional state was being coldly analysed and computed for future reference.

'Your sister intrigues me,' Drew commented at last, his long, tanned fingers toying with a slender brass paper-knife on his blotter. 'She seems a very. . .*strong-minded* young lady, considering she's only twenty-one?'

'Yes. Fiona is a great one for "positive thinking",' Charlotte blurted out, bitterly, before she had time to check her words. 'She'll go far.'

'I gather the two of you don't exactly get on?'

'I wouldn't say that. . .' She hesitated, avoiding his probing eyes, cursing her unguarded outburst. The truth was she hadn't realised quite how poor their relationship was until now. Superficially, they'd got along fine for years. Maybe nothing had cropped up to test their feelings towards each other, until now.

'Sibling rivalry?' He sounded as if he was hazarding a mocking guess.

She shrugged. 'It's probably my fault—I'm beginning to think I'm not very good at relationships,' she said stiffly, and Drew nodded slowly, his pale yellow eyes curiously unsettling as he scrutinised her face.

'Or maybe you and Fiona are just carrying on your parents' fight?'

'Spare me the Freudian analyses, please,' she countered tautly. 'Fee and I are totally different people. Just because we're sisters, it doesn't mean we're destined to agree on everything!'

'True. . .' Drew appeared to consider the matter at some length. 'Fiona certainly seems to have her head screwed on in some respects.' He sounded thoughtful, almost admiring.

Charlotte stared at him numbly. Did he find Fee attractive? Were the vibrations she sensed emanating from her sister being picked up and returned by Drew? It felt as if someone were slowly turning a knife in her stomach. Surely, surely, she wasn't letting Drew affect her again, as he had before? He meant nothing to her now—nothing, she reminded herself brutally. And she'd better make her indifference absolutely clear. She could think of a no more humiliating scenario than competing with her sister for the affections of Drew Meredith!

She gripped the window-ledge, her eyes fixed on the bobbing yachts below, only distantly aware of how the sun had struggled through the stormy grey sky and was flashing brilliantly off the rows of aluminium masts.

'Fee is certainly a realist. She doesn't let sentiment interfere with her decisions,' she agreed at last, with only a slight shake in her voice, 'but I can be a realist as well. I admit I have a sentimental attachment to my father's boatyard, but I know I can't change my father's will. I can't argue with him about it—ask him why he did it. I have to accept you are the major shareholder,' she drew a deep breath, 'but I truly believe the business can be viable again. Will you at least give me a chance to prove what I can do with it?'

She kept her back to him, hardly daring to turn

and look at his face, so it made her jump when he spoke from close behind her.

'You're asking me to cough up the money to cover the debts, as well as investing in this new boat-building scheme of yours?'

'Yes.'

'That cost you a lot of pride, didn't it?' His voice was deep, tinged with an inflexion she couldn't quite place. Not sarcasm this time, not mockery. What?

'It's not easy having to plead for favours, if that's what you mean!' she admitted forcibly, turning now to stare up into his dark face, and fighting the ignominious wave of weakness brought on by his proximity.

'Especially from me?'

'You know the answer to that!' She gazed at him bitterly, colour seeping into her face. 'Why do you keep harping on about the past? Surely you got enough sadistic enjoyment from it all five years ago?'

'Sadistic enjoyment?' One black eyebrow arched sardonically, but his expression darkened. 'That's a quaint description of my feelings.'

'Have you got a better one?'

For a long time Drew said nothing, his brooding stillness reminiscent of a sleepy lion, the tawny-yellow irises mesmerising and infinitely disturbing. The silence seemed to stretch on forever, until her nerves were taut.

'I was never any good at explaining my feelings,' he murmured finally, his deep voice slightly hoarser. He lifted a supple brown hand to trace the tense line of her jaw, making her flinch involuntarily. 'That's something we may have in common. We're not very good at relationships.'

She was drowning in that gaze, her heart thudding unevenly. She might not be one hundred per cent successful at relationships, but Drew Meredith was a great deal worse than she was, she decided. A more barricaded personality would be hard to find in a lifetime's search. He was cynical, embittered, unreachable. Maybe he'd mellowed just a fraction over the last five years, maybe he didn't seem to be quite such a wild loner—but that was just time smoothing the surface, knocking off the rough edges. Underneath he was still the same abrasive character—the way he was behaving over the boat-yard proved that, if nothing else. . .

His fingers cupped her chin for a second, then moved lightly round her neck to the sensitive nape, beneath her hair, and for a moment she thought she would cry out with the surge of reaction to his touch. Instinctively, for self-protection, she stepped back-wards, cringing away from him until she was pressed up hard against the window-sill, and the fear in her eyes must have suddenly communicated itself to him because abruptly he dropped his hand, his eyes hardening.

'All right. You've got a month, Charlotte,' he said curtly, taking her by surprise, 'for sentiment's sake only. After that, market forces dictate our policy. Agreed?'

Still reeling from the insidious effect of his touch,

she flattened the small surge of elation. She was certainly scraping the barrel if *this* concession made her feel optimistic! Still, it was a start. The elation refused to completely disperse.

'A month isn't very long,' she persisted disbelievingly, her eyes locked with his, fighting the idiotic flutters of panic in her stomach, 'It takes about six months to build a forty-foot trimaran! At what stage will I be deemed to have succeeded?'

'Get the order signed and sealed,' Drew suggested abruptly. 'I'll sort out the buildings insurance.'

She tried ruthlessly to check her surge of joy, aware of the irony of the situation. Of all the people in the world to act as her reluctant saviour, Drew Meredith was about the least likely, and the least welcome.

'Thank you.' It sounded stiff, false. Drew's wide mouth twisted in wry amusement, and his gaze dropped lazily from her eyes, lingering on the determined set of her lips, then travelling slowly and deliberately down the full length of her body, lingering on the soft swell of her breasts, and the boyish curve of her waist and hips in the figure-hugging denims.

'I hope you'll demonstrate a suitable degree of gratitude?' He sounded deeply cynical.

'What do you mean?' The question was jerked out of her, her expression so horrified he began to laugh, giving her another reprehensible urge to hit him.

'Maybe you'll be a little more amenable, more open to reason? You're not exactly an easy partner to work with, Charlotte. What did you think I meant?' His last words were laced with mocking innuendo.

'Drew. . .don't play around with me!' Their eyes clashed silently, but he was still mocking her, the amused light masking his feelings.

'Surely when it comes to "playing around", you're hardly in a position to criticise? Don't forget I've had a taste of your fickle nature.' Ignoring the rush of dark colour in her face, he glanced coolly down at his watch, his expression bland. 'I've got to work this morning, unfortunately. Five of my skippers are off with the flu, so I'm taking a couple of sailing classes. How about lunch?'

'Lunch?' she repeated idiotically, a tumult of panic in her stomach, as she tried to decipher his meaning. She was being paranoid, surely, if she thought Drew meant to ravish her in his lunch hour as a means of extracting payment for his generosity? Her vivid imagination was worthy of a Victorian melodrama!

'I'll pick you up from the boatyard, at one o'clock.'

She glared at him coldly. 'I'm sorry—I'm lunching with a friend today.' She began moving cautiously towards the door.

'Dinner, then.'

'I'm sorry. I'll be far too tired to go out for dinner tonight——'

'Too tired to sweet-talk a suitable naval architect into supervising the Smithson project?'

Her mouth had been open ready to counter any efforts at persuasion, but she shut it abruptly, compressing her lips in mutinous silence. Slowly, she shook her head, and Drew's answering smile made her want to hit him again.

'I'll call for you at eight.'

He turned away dismissively, returning to some paperwork on his desk, and Charlotte drew a deep, calming breath as she quietly left the office and made her way slowly down the spiral metal staircase winding down the outside of the building to the quayside, conscious of having been out-manoeuvred yet again. Drew seemed determined to inflict his will on her, she reflected rebelliously. And somehow she'd managed to land up in the unenviable position of being in his debt. She was beginning to think that her previous low opinion of him had been wildly conservative. He wasn't merely a cold-blooded autocrat, he was a snake, a rat. . . He was enjoying himself, giving orders, making her sweat over the fate of her father's business, condescending to allow her a month to prove herself, charming Fiona into siding with him. . .

She seethed for the rest of the morning, and not even lunch at Susie's, with the entertainment of the four-year-old twins thrown in, could appease her simmering resentment. Her friend was diplomatic enough not to probe too deeply into Charlotte's tension, but the Shalmouth grapevine was active enough for her to be aware of most of the details of Jonathan Wells's legacy. Susie's bright brown eyes

were eloquent with curiosity and sympathy, and
Charlotte was glad, for once, of the distracting antics
of the children, which made coherent conversation
impossible. She gratefully ate the mouth-watering
quiche and salad and crunchy French bread, and
refused the temptation of wine. She wanted to keep
a clear head for her afternoon in the boatyard, and
for the evening ahead with Drew.

By the time she got through the rest of the day,
her emotions were snarled up as tightly as a knotted
ball of wool, not helped by the moody, lovelorn
presence of Delia in the office, and Geoff's pessi-
mistic reaction to every fresh problem that arose.

Back in the solitary silence of the basement flat,
she took one glare at her tense white face in the
mirror and decided it was time to take a grip on
herself. Stripping off her clothes, and pinning her
dark curls high on top of her head, she turned the
bath taps on full, and poured a lavish dollop of
musk-perfumed bubble bath under the rush of running water. The heady fragrance rose up to meet
her, warm and spicy and predictably comforting.
Sinking her long, slender limbs beneath the silky
bubbles, she closed her eyes and let her mind drift.

Life seemed to have altered so rapidly, and she'd
had so much to think about, she'd hardly had time
to meditate on the changes. A few weeks ago, she'd
been fighting her way through the London rush hour
on the Tube each morning to the rarefied world of
million-pound masterpieces, and priceless porcelain.
Now it felt as if the years had abruptly rolled back,

flipping her back in time. She was in Shalmouth again, the town of her childhood. This was where she'd grown up, made friendships, spent endless happy hours racing her dinghy around the buoys in the estuary with Colin, and Susie, and Tim Fennel, and the rest of her sailing club friends. An image of Colin's expressive, freckled face swam into her mind, and she felt a pang of regret. He'd gone off to university too, after that fateful summer, and she hardly ever saw him. She'd remained very fond of Colin, in spite of the tensions on board the *Menorquina*, and afterwards at Antonia's villa in Menorca. She hated losing touch with old friends.

Lazily, she searched out the sponge and squeezed soapy water over her stomach, eyeing the smooth, flat expanse of pale skin, indented by the neat dip of her navel, stretching tautly down to the triangle of dark hair at its base. She had a dancer's body, from the years of early ballet training which had been one of her few concessions to her mother's wishes. But there were times when she felt as if her body didn't really belong to her. There had been a time when she'd deeply envied Fiona's luscious curves, but when she'd developed her own, admittedly to a less spectacular degree, she'd had conflicting feelings about this new femininity. Men sometimes said extravagant things about her, but she found it impossible to take them seriously. Their words seemed to apply to some other girl's body, not her own. They might wax poetic about the leanness of her muscles, the firm swell of her breasts, her slender grace, but inside she felt as straight and flat and sexless as a young boy. . .

The vague panic started forming, deep inside her again, and abruptly she sat up, bubbles streaming down her shoulders, just as a loud hammering sounded on the front door of the flat. With trembling fingers she grabbed a towel and began rubbing herself dry, and the knocking began again just as she was thrusting her arms into a pale aqua towelling robe and running on bare feet across the cold varnished floorboards of the hall.

Flinging open the door, she stared in stunned surprise at the tall, overpoweringly masculine shape of Drew, in battered tan flying jacket, loose cream shirt and rust cords, one shoulder propped nonchalantly against the door-jamb.

'Oh, it's you!' she exclaimed involuntarily, clutching the robe around her like a shield. 'What are you doing here? It's only seven o'clock!'

Drew checked his watch with an air of calm surprise. 'Sorry I'm early. But I think you'd better let me in—you'll catch a chill standing at the door like that.'

He was looking at her bare toes, and still-wet legs, and she hastily stepped back to let him in, shivering at the cold draught as Drew pushed the front door closed behind him.

'Not exactly cosy, is it?' Drew was gazing round the bare sitting-room, shedding his leather jacket slowly, his expression wry.

'It's quite adequate. My father had rather spartan

tastes.' She gestured abruptly to the drinks table. 'Help yourself to a whisky or something. I'd better go and get dressed. . .'

'Yes. . .' Drew's gaze was brooding as he flicked his eyes over her '. . . I think you'd better. Don't worry—I know my way around. I've drunk whisky here before, with your father.'

She withdrew hurriedly, her whole body tingling in reaction to that piercing appraisal. In the privacy of the bedroom she smoothed on some musk body lotion, and then sorted through the clothes recently retrieved from her London bedsit. Judging from Drew's smart but casual appearance, she wasn't expected to dress up too much, she decided, hurriedly opting for the grey crêpe culottes, French-cut to slide close over the bottom yet fall in elegant pleats to mid-calf. She tucked a loose, white silk shirt into the narrow waistband, and added soft grey leather boots, inspecting the result doubtfully in the mirror.

Her reflection gazed back at her, the solemn white oval of her face accentuated by the riotous cloud of dark curls. She looked too pale, she judged impatiently. Drew would start interrogating her again about working too hard, and she hated being forced on the defensive. On sudden inspiration she knotted a brightly patterned grey and crimson silk scarf loosely round her neck, and brushed some blusher on her cheekbones. That was better. It was hard to exude radiant self-confidence when you resembled a wraith.

'You look nice,' Drew commented blandly, as she joined him in the sitting-room. She was mortified to find herself blushing.

'Thanks. Would you like another drink?'

'Not if I'm driving. Shall we go?'

She shrugged and nodded, collecting her grey sheepskin jacket and following him out into the blustery cold night.

It was trying hard to snow, sudden gusts of fine white sleet pattering against the windscreen.

'Where are we going? Nowhere too pricey, since I've every intention of going Dutch,' she announced, as they headed out along the coast road.

Drew said nothing for a few moments, then expelled his breath in a long, exasperated sigh. 'Charlotte, can we call a truce?' he said bluntly, glancing sideways at her clenched face. 'I accept that past events are liable to place a certain. . .constraint on our relationship, but this hostility is starting to irritate me!'

'Aren't you mistaking hostility for independence?'

'I don't think so. In any case, there's a limit to how independent you can be in your present position.'

'There you go agan!' she burst out, abandoning all attempts at maintaining a polite distance. 'You just can't resist turning the screws, can you? How could I ever have been naïve enough to *admire* you!'

'Never put another human being on a pedestal, Charlotte. They have a nasty habit of falling off!'

'Drew, going out to dinner tonight was *your* idea,

not mine!' she seethed, fists clenched, 'I'm beginning to wonder if suffering your company is too high a price to pay for saving my father's boatyard!'

'Are you?' There was a sardonic twist to his mouth, and she suddenly realised that the BMW was slowing down, pulling off the road into a deserted lay-by. Her heart was already thudding fast from anger, but now it was thundering for quite a different reason. Cutting the engine, Drew turned purposefully in his seat, and smiled humourlessly at her flushed face and mutinous mouth.

'Are you really so averse to my company?' he persisted softly, the pale eyes disturbingly piercing, the pupils seeming to expand and darken his gaze even as she stared warily back at him. 'Or are you just playing your curious little games again?'

She found she was breathless, her voice almost refusing to function. 'I don't know what you mean.'

'I'll demonstrate, then, shall I?' He didn't wait for an answer, his left arm snaking across the back of her seat, his right hand moving possessively around her waist, his fingers splaying over the pounding of her heart beneath her ribcage. Charlotte froze, utterly incapable of either speech or movement, as Drew's dark head bent closer, and his lips moved with subtle, persuasive exploration over hers.

CHAPTER FIVE

THE astonishing sensations unleashed by the texture of Drew's cool lips moving over Charlotte's mouth brought her hands up to clutch his broad shoulders, in a jerky reflex action. She tried to protest, but the sound was commuted to a moan somewhere deep in her throat. A shudder of passion rocked her, shooting heat through her whole body, and the heat seemed to transfer itself to Drew, because his restraint abruptly departed, his mouth parting her lips urgently in a deep, searching thrust for possession, his tongue probing the soft warmth of her mouth. He tasted of whisky, and he smelt, as he always had done, of an elusive, faintly spicy aftershave, and of the sea, an indescribable blend of aromas which sent her senses scattering wildly into chaos.

A sob rose in her throat, but it was a confused sob, combining outrage with such a lance of desire she tightened her grasp convulsively, crumpling the supple leather of his jacket in her fingers, no longer sure if she was pushing him away, or straining him closer. Emotion clouded her mind until only the hardness and strength of his shoulders under her fingers, and the warm heady smell of his skin, seemed real. A vast silence seemed to have enveloped her, the only sound the slight creak of the leather jacket as Drew moved, and the laboured sound of their breathing.

His mouth moved down, leaving her swollen lips and straying lower to kiss her throat, and his caressing hands became more demanding as he stroked her burning skin through the fine silk of her blouse beneath the sheepskin jacket, slowly circling beneath the tender jut of her breasts, sending a terrifying flood of arousal through her lower body.

'Drew. . .no. . .don't, oh, please. . .' What was she begging for? The brief gasp for air brought no relief from the unbearable excitement shimmering through her limbs.

'Don't fight me. . .' His voice sounded muffled and unfamiliar, thick with emotion, his breath mingling with her own, and she felt a fresh shock of intimacy as his long fingers stroked up over her ribs and discovered the rigid nub of her left breast beneath the silken covering, its peak unashamedly swollen and aching for his caress. The sob of panic burst from her throat then, and fight him she did, in earnest, writhing and scratching like a wildcat. Drew released her from his arms, catching her flailing wrists and holding them tightly in his hands, his face dark and intense as he scrutinised her face in the dim interior light of the car.

'Relax. . .' he sounded far from relaxed himself, his deep voice tight with some unfamiliar emotion. '. . .game over.'

He held her wrists until the tension had gone out of her, then released her slowly, turning back to start the engine, his profile rigid. His voice sounded distant when he spoke again.

'I'm starving. Let's go and eat, shall we?'

'I'm not hungry. . .' Her own voice seemed to be coming from somewhere else as well, and she lay her head weakly back against the head-rest as they drove, closing her eyes and waiting miserably for the flood-tide of emotion to drain away.

'Not even for paella?' The car slowed down as Drew spoke, and she opened her eyes to see the yellow and white striped awning of the famous seafood restaurant at Bedleigh, with its glass conservatory looking across the dark stretch of the estuary towards the light-spangled headland in the distance. She sat up quickly, her face growing hot with indignation.

'Drew, I told you, I want to pay my share! This place is way above my pocket.'

Drew turned swiftly to face her, taking hold of her arms in a none too gentle grip and giving her a slight shake.

'Truce, Charlotte. Remember?' he grated roughly. 'If you think I'm going to suffer a hamburger and a thick shake just to save your pride, think again!'

'I wasn't suggesting a hamburger. . .' she began stiffly, but his wide mouth twitched in weary amusement as he searched her wooden expression.

'Charlotte. . .Charlotte. . .' He seemed aware that he was crushing her narrow wrists in his fingers and abruptly released her, lifting her hands and inspecting the dull red marks which slowly rose on her skin. 'I'm sorry—I didn't intend to bruise your skin. . .but do me a favour, just for tonight, stop arguing and do as you're told,' he finished quietly, getting out of the car and circling the bonnet to open her door. 'I remember you like paella. Pepe here doesn't quite match the restaurant on the quayside at Ciudadela, but he comes a close second. Let's pretend we're friends and go and have dinner, shall we?'

'I don't appear to have much choice in the matter,' she murmured through her teeth, as Drew propelled her through the door into the ecstatic greeting of Pepe, who took their coats, shepherded them to the best table in the corner by the vast picture window, and produced velvet-covered menus with a sensual flourish.

'*Un momento*, I shall light your candle for you, Señor Meredith. For an evening *muy romántico, sí*?' The Spaniard's dark eyes swept knowledgeably over Charlotte's hectically flushed cheeks and dilated eyes, and he gave a small nod of satisfaction.

'*Muy romántico*, Pepe,' Drew agreed wryly. '*Muchas gracias!*'

The pink candle flickered into suitably romantic action between them, and Charlotte glared at Drew through the golden halo of light.

'*Muy romántico*, indeed!' she seethed softly. 'I've a good mind to enlighten the poor deluded man!'

'If you don't relax, you'll end up with peptic

ulcers,' Drew commented lightly, turning his attention to the wine waiter. 'I don't know how you feel, but I'd prefer a dry French white.'

'Yes, that suits me.' She avoided his eyes, still much too conscious of the shameful arousal of her body, the weak melting of her stomach at the memory of his caresses. Self-consciously she adjusted the scarf, trying to hide the stubborn thrust of her breasts through the thin silk blouse. Drew was watching her, his narrowed eyes gleaming pale gold in the candle-light.

'Stop staring at me!' she muttered furiously, colour washing over her again at his expression.

'If I didn't know better, I'd be quite taken in by all those virginal blushes.'

'I thought you mentioned a truce? If you keep on like this I'll end up smashing this expensive bottle of wine over your head!'

'You're right.' The taunting light only partly faded from his eyes. 'We're not doing too well, are we? We'd better make certain subjects taboo. Personal lives, mores and morals are definitely out. So's the boatyard. We'd better choose a neutral topic and stick to it.'

'Sailing?' she suggested, with a stab of amusement despite the fraught situation. 'The life and times of Bertolt Brecht? The operas of Verdi?'

The hard mouth twisted. 'Is that a direct attack on my limited range of interests?'

'No. Although it proves I've got a good memory too. You and Colin used to make me feel a hopeless philistine with your knowledgeable discussions on music and literature.'

'Surely not? You used to contribute the occasional witticism, as I recall. Talking with you and Colin was rather like conversing with a particularly well-rehearsed comedy act!'

There was a short silence, and she stared at him warily. This was awful, like playing chess in the dark. No matter which way the conversation turned, they always seemed to come back to the same point of contention.

The awkward moment was relieved by the arrival of Pepe with side-table and equipment to cook the paella, drawing interested glances from the other guests in the conservatory. She had a sudden vivid memory of the night she and Drew had eaten this, in Menorca, at the pavement café at the old port of Ciudadela. They'd moored the *Menorquina* right by their chosen eating place, stepped off the deck and into the noisy, crowded darkness of the quayside. There had been five of them, outwardly relaxed and laughing, inwardly hiding tensions and uncertainties. Antonia and her boyfriend Griff, Colin, Drew, and herself. . .

'You've got a glazed look about you,' Drew said levelly, snapping her attention back to the present, pouring more wine into her glass and topping up his own with mineral water. 'I wish you'd make an effort. Pepe will think I'm losing my touch!'

Her eyes flashed. So Drew regularly brought women here, did he? That shouldn't surprise her.

Delia? Or the mystery owner of the satin nightdress?
The pain twisted deeper inside her.

'Do you still see Colin?' he enquired evenly, after
another endless pause.

'Not often. He went to study English at Oxford,
and he's teaching now, at a boy's boarding-school in
Norfolk. I wish we'd kept in touch, though. . . I was
very fond of Colin.'

Drew's face was unreadable. 'That's one way of
putting it. Was he a more co-operative lover than I
turned out to be?'

'I thought we were going to stick to neutral
subjects?' It was an effort to form the words, she
was so seized up inside at Drew's casual probing.
But this was her own fault—she'd brought Colin
into the conversation, either accidentally or through
some unconscious urge to torture herself.

'We were. But neither of us seem very good at
small talk, do we? We've sat here in silence for the
last five minutes.'

This was true enough. Drew had never been one
for idle chatter, his preference for his own company
on months of solitary sailing trips evidence enough,
but the episode in the car had robbed her of her
normal capacity for social chit-chat. Her composure
felt badly rocked—not so much by Drew's arrogance
in kissing her the way he had, but by her own eager
response to it. It was five years since she'd felt such
a searing physical hunger for someone—and the fact
that it was still Drew Meredith who could arouse

such feelings inside her was almost too ironic to believe.

'We need to talk about it, Charlotte. . .' he said softly, making her heart lurch clumsily in her chest.

'No! We don't!' She spoke in a low, rapid undertone. 'I understand perfectly how things are—you made yourself blindingly clear at the time. The last thing we want now is a post-mortem!'

'Charlotte. . .' his face darkened, his gaze coldly critical on her tense face. '. . .you must know how impossible the whole situation was. . .you were little more than a child! I'd promised your father I'd take care of you!'

'Drew, can we please drop this?'

'No. I think the time has come for some straight talking, Charlotte. You're treating me like the original black-hearted brigand—but you were the one who jumped from my bed into Colin's, for pity's sake!'

The colour drained from her face, and they faced each other in the ensuing silence, the candle-light flickering on wide green eyes and narrowed amber ones, highlighting the cruel harshness of Drew's dark face, and the pale, expressionless oval of Charlotte's.

She started to stand up, blindly in need of escape, but he reached across the table, pinioning her to her seat, with a sharp shake of his head.

'Sit still. You're not walking out on me, you're going to stay here and eat Pepe's delicious paella, and if you like we'll talk about something a little more relevant to the present.'

She subsided, reluctantly, her eyes wary. 'Well, at least you admit the past has no relevance!'

'Not entirely what I meant. . .' Drew leaned back in his chair, his eyes holding hers very steadily. 'We're both products of our own experiences, aren't we? And in our case, products of our shared experiences as well?'

Pepe was hovering around the steaming frying-pan beside them, signalling that the paella was almost ready, and the wine waiter moved soundlessly up to refill her wine glass. She noticed Drew abruptly shook his head when the bottle moved towards his glass, and she realised she was drinking far more than he was. Nervous tension, she deduced, resolving to pull herself together and make an effort to converse normally.

'So if we're all products of our own experiences, what kind of a product are you?' she enquired brightly, as Pepe served huge portions of the rice and seafood on to their plates. 'Mmm!' She put a forkful of the paella into her mouth, and directed one of her rare, dazzling smiles at Pepe. 'This is superb! *Buenísima*, Pepe!'

The Spaniard's face flushed with pleasure, and he gave a delighted bow, his laughing eyes darting from one to the other as he left them to enjoy his masterpiece.

'I'd say I'm a fairly flawed product.' Drew's eyes had hardened slightly as he'd witnessed her instant conquest of Pepe. 'I suspect certain aspects of my life have left their mark. . . I never felt too enthusiastic about the circumstances of my birth, for example. I get very hot under the collar about unwanted babies. And there's a part of me that looks very cynically on the concept of motherhood and the caring woman.'

'I see. . .' She hesitated, the subtle tensions of her own childhood seeming tame by comparison with Drew's disquieting start in the world. 'So you don't think much of the female of the species?' Why was she asking the question, she wondered, when she already knew the answer?

'Let's just say my experience in life hasn't made me the most trusting man in the world.'

'So you've never married?' The words just seemed to tumble out, as if now that she'd crossed the initial pain barrier she couldn't stop this masochistic desire to hurt herself.

Drew paused with a forkful of paella halfway to his mouth, his gaze lidded. 'I didn't say that.'

Charlotte remembered the pink satin nightdress, and felt slightly sick. 'You're married?' It came out as a hoarse whisper, and she hurriedly cleared her throat.

'I was.'

'Recently? I mean. . .since we sailed to Menorca?'

He shook his head, his mouth twisting mockingly. 'No.'

She sipped some more wine, avoiding his eyes. 'The marriage didn't work out?'

'Evidently.' Drew put down his fork, and tipped his chair back slightly, his expression forbidding.

'What went wrong?' She wasn't sure how she was finding the nerve to ask so many personal questions. Maybe it was the wine. The look in Drew's eyes was making her grow hot.

'Just about everything that can go wrong in a relationship. I haven't asked what went wrong between you and Colin.'

'I wasn't married to Colin,' she countered lightly, her lashes veiling her eyes as Drew's piercing gaze lanced through her.

'But he was pretty keen on you. And in my book sleeping with someone is a fairly heavy commitment.'

Charlotte's green eyes were suddenly cold. 'Situations are not always what they appear to be. Just because you were too cynical and grubby-minded to believe Colin and I were just friends——'

'Just *friends*?' Drew's echo was sardonic. 'You're trying to tell me that what happened on the night Antonia's parents went across to Marbella was just a friendly game? It won't work, Charlotte. I *saw* you and Colin together—or had you conveniently blocked that little scene from your memory?'

She gazed back at him speechlessly, wishing she could do just that. But the harrowing moment came creeping back into her mind, making her stomach churn painfully. Drew had been sleeping on board the *Menorquina*, but using the shower facilities at the villa, and he'd come over earlier than usual, opened Colin's and Griff's bedroom door to collect his soap bag and towel, and seen her half naked in bed with Colin. . . The evidence had been fairly damning, she supposed, in the rational light of retrospection. She lifted her chin defiantly.

'I can't see any point trying to justify that to you again. If you didn't believe me five years ago, you're unlikely to believe me now, and to be quite honest I really couldn't care less whether you believe me or not!'

'Let me see now. . .' Drew sounded lazily amused. 'I was asked to believe that Antonia's parents had gone out for the night, Antonia and Griff were so impatient to consummate their teenage love-affair they forced you and Colin to share a bedroom together to give them a clear run? Even though there was another empty bedroom in the villa, all that night?'

'Stop it, Drew. I don't want to talk about this— it's. . .it's sordid and horrible!'

He arched a dark eyebrow in mock surprise. 'Not necessarily—young love is a notoriously impulsive and passionate affair, don't you agree? The only sordid and horrible part as far as I was concerned was that you'd just declared undying love for me, the previous week!'

'And you made it brutally clear you thought I was an overgrown schoolgirl without a brain in her head!

So of course I leapt into bed with Colin on the rebound?'

'I don't think I put it like that——'

'You didn't need to say it in so many words!' She managed a cool smile at him, the masochistic process of talking to Drew about the past seeming to leave her strangely calmer, clearer-headed. 'And anyway, thank goodness we all grow up eventually. Don't worry about offending me now—I'm older and wiser and quite immune to your dubious charms!'

'Charlotte. . .' Drew leaned forward across the table, taking her hand in his and examining it with what seemed an undue amount of attention. 'When I kissed you a little while ago, in the car, I couldn't help getting the impression you weren't entirely. . .immune to my "dubious charms".'

His touch seemed to burn her. She snatched her hand back, cradling it stupidly in her lap. 'I assure you I am! Physical. . .physical feelings have nothing to do with. . .caring for someone, do they?' Her cheeks were on fire, and there was an irritating prickle of moisture in her eyes which she blinked furiously away. 'After all, look how fickle I am! You've just said so yourself!'

'Charlotte. . .' For once, Drew looked visibly disturbed, raking a none too steady hand through his black curls and eyeing her uncertainly. He stared at her for a long moment, then looked away, lifting a hand to summon the waiter. 'Shall we have some pudding?'

She shook her head.

'Coffee, then.'

There was another silence as they waited for the table to be cleared and their coffee to arrive, and Charlotte pleated the tablecloth between her finger and thumb, staring out of the window through the darkness at the glitter of gold and silver lights dotted over the distant headland. It had begun to rain, now, the wind lashing the drops against the glass in a bleak tattoo.

'I was going to talk to you tonight about where you're intending to live,' Drew said at last, as the coffee was poured. 'Presumably you're going to have cash-flow problems for a while?'

'I'll manage.'

'What's that supposed to mean? You'll start looking for a place to live when you leave you father's flat on Sunday night?'

She was silent, loath to admit that she really hadn't had the time or energy to devote to that particular problem. 'I won't be sleeping under the railway bridge. There's always the couch at Susie's, until I sort something out. . .'

'Or Fiona?'

'She's only got a studio flat, so that's no good,' she said dismissively, draining the last of her black coffee.

'And you wouldn't want to live with Fiona, in any case?'

She shrugged. 'I'm very fond of Fee. But I can't pretend we always see eye to eye. I'll manage, anyway. I don't care if I have to camp out in the sail-loft at the boatyard——'

'Under the leaking roof?'

Drew rose abruptly, signalling the waiter and unceremoniously settling the bill and hustling her out of the restaurant, into the lashing rain. His air of cool preoccupation was daunting.

'Why the tearing hurry? Can't you stand my company a second longer?' she enquired sarcastically.

'I've got something to show you,' was all he would supply, practically pushing her into the car.

They took the coast road, then took the turning along the side of the estuary, and it didn't take her long to suspect where they were heading.

'Where are we going exactly?' She already knew, deep down, and her stomach was in a fresh set of knots at the unwelcome prospect of visiting Drew's house again, especially at this time of night, when the same autocratic excuse to make use of a guest room could be pulled readily out of a hat.

'You'll see.'

'Drew, I'm not a little child!' she ground out impatiently. 'You don't have to play games with me!'

'Technically, I'm your boss at the moment,' Drew murmured thoughtfully, 'so maybe you'd better get used to humouring me.'

'Like hell I will,' she muttered under her breath, subsiding in exasperated silence until the car slowed and turned into the long, tree-lined drive to Drew's house.

The house looked different tonight, with lights glowing through the rows of arched, leaded windows, gables and chimneys jutting up against the night sky. Ultra-modern heat-sensor lights sprang abruptly into action as the car drew closer, floodlighting the whole sweep of the drive. She hadn't noticed these things the other night, when Drew had brought her here from the hospital after her father's death. Maybe she'd been too numb and shocked to absorb her surroundings.

'Authentic sixteenth-century floodlighting?' she murmured, with a deadpan glance at Drew.

'I had to fix those for Mrs Bolton. My housekeeper has a nervous disposition. That's why the whole manor house is lit up like a bloody funfair. She costs me a fortune in electricity.'

Charlotte was climbing out of the car warily, hiding her sudden smile. She felt as if invisible antennae were quivering in readiness for Drew's next move. 'It is rather a remote spot,' she said thoughtfully, looking round. 'I can imagine it might daunt some people.'

'Would it scare you?'

She stood still for a moment, and listened to the eerie silence. It had stopped raining now, and the wide stretch of estuary on the far side of the house was calm. The quiet was as dense as the darkness beyond the trees, with only occasional hoots and

muffled squeaks to prove that owls and bats were
alert and wide awake in the night.

'No, it wouldn't scare me,' she said at last. 'I
found London pretty scary—city nightlife is much
more dangerous than the country variety!'

'At least we agree on something.' Drew's tone was
bland. His feet on the gravel broke the silence as he
moved to take her arm. She stiffened instinctively,
but he was guiding her away from the main stone
archway to the manor, leading her instead around
the side of the house, and along a dark, rutted lane
which sloped down towards the shore for about fifty
yards until they came to a small, whitewashed cottage, standing end-ways on to the beach. She
watched in cautious silence while he produced a key,
unlocked the door and flicked on some lights.

'Come on in,' he called over his shoulder, as she
remained on the doorstep. 'This is Cormorant
Cottage—Mrs Bolton's convinced there's a resident
ghost, but you don't strike me as the type to be
nervous of the supernatural!'

'Charming,' she murmured drily, but she stepped
inside nevertheless, drawn in by curiosity, staring
round with objective detachment. Uneven grey flag-
stone floors had been recently polished, and Chinese
rugs were dotted about. There were original, black-
ened beams criss-crossing the whitewashed walls.
She caught a glimpse of pretty floral sofas in the
sitting-room, and had to abruptly put the brakes on
her imagination when she pictured a sleepy Persian
cat like Beth and Jocelyn's Magnus, stretched out in

front of the fire-blackened ingle-nook fireplace.
There were even dried flowers clumped together in
a glorious mass of hyacinth blue and mauve, and
cream and white, in a basket on a window-sill.
Through the leaded windows she could see the dull
sheen of moonlight on the calm surface of the
estuary.

'Who lives here? It's not as old as the manor, is
it?'

'No. It's probably seventeenth century. My—er—
a friend of mine furnished and decorated it for me.
She's an interior decorator. She lived here for a
while, then she had to go abroad. Mrs Bolton lived
here after that, but my housekeeper is very prone to
hearing strange things that go bump in the night. . .'

Drew's tone was laconic, and as he was speaking
he'd strolled lazily into the sitting-room, and bent
down to a drinks table, ready laid with whisky
decanter and glasses, on the left of the deep ingle-
nook fireplace. He poured a measure of whisky into
two glasses, and held one out to her, his expression
deadpan.

She shook her head, eyeing him levelly, her own
heart bumping rather like one of Mrs Bolton's
imaginary ghosts.

'If no one lives here, why are there whisky and
glasses in the sitting-room? Why have you brought
me here, Drew?'

Drew's eyes were narrowed pensively. 'We forgot
to discuss your Smithson contract,' he said quietly,
switching subjects without warning. 'But you need

the advice of a naval architect, and you certainly can't afford to pay for one. So. . . I'll volunteer my services free of charge on one condition. . .'

Suspicion was growing, and she stared at him disbelievingly. 'Go on. . .what's the condition?'

'That you forget these hare-brained schemes about sleeping on couches, or roughing it on the sail-loft floor. If you're fool enough to contemplate spending even one night alone in the boatyard, that's enough for me! I owe it to your father that you at least have a safe roof over your head. This place is yours, rent-free, for as long as you need it.' He saw her mutinous expression and added sharply, 'And since we've already spent the entire evening arguing, I'm in no mood to start all over again!'

CHAPTER SIX

CHARLOTTE sat down abruptly on one of the blue and cream flowered sofas, and gazed at Drew in stunned silence for a while. She felt totally confused, which made her angrier than ever.

'I think I'm beginning to understand. . .' she said at last, holding out her hand almost absently for the glass of whisky, and taking a large, inelegant gulp. 'You're feeling guilty about planning to bulldoze my father's boatyard to the ground, and you're salving your conscience by offering me a free roof over my head?'

Drew's expression darkened. 'If that's how you want to interpret it.'

She was silent again, considering the situation

'Why do I get the feeling you're enjoying every minute of my new charity status?' she asked at last, controlling her anger with a supreme effort.

'Don't be ridiculous!'

'Then why this avuncular concern for my welfare?' she snapped back, glancing around at the luxurious interior of the cottage with a fresh surge of anger. The cottage was irresistible, and Drew must know it. He was putting her in an impossible position, beholden to him, and apparently forced into submission by him. As revenge for imagined wrongs of the past, Cormorant Cottage was a novel method of punishment. Most people she knew would pay the earth to live here. . .yet Drew was implying that, if she didn't live here, she'd lose her chance to save Wells Boats. . .?

'There's nothing avuncular about my feelings towards you.'

'Then what?' She glared at him, green eyes suddenly flashing fire. 'What have you got to gain from being so *generous*?'

Drew's gaze was lidded, his expression ambiguous, and she gave a shaky laugh.

'You're definitely *not* lusting after me!' she said derisively. 'At least I've learned my lessons on that score!'

Drew's eyes were revealing nothing of his feelings. He poured himself another Scotch, and downed it with scant regard for the social niceties. 'Stop being so aggressive and argumentative, Charlotte. Can't you just accept a straightforward offer of help?'

'It's difficult, coming from you.' Fresh fury welled inside her as the full implications of Drew's 'offer' began to sink in. 'Are you seriously suggesting that you'll only help me on the Smithson trimaran project if I accept your charity?'

He shrugged. 'Call it charity, or you could look on it as a temporary loan. But yes, I suppose that's the deal.'

'But *why*?' she burst out, genuinely bewildered by the gleam of determination in his eyes.

He raised an eyebrow sardonically. 'I can't pretend I won't enjoy watching you swallow that damned pride of yours!'

She was on her feet, jerked upright like a wildcat. '*My* pride?' she exploded. 'That's rich coming from you! You're so damned haughty and arrogant you can hardly see down your long nose!'

'We're sinking to the level of insults again, are we?' The long nose under discussion flared fractionally around the nostrils as Drew's temper began to visibly fray.

'No, we're on to some home truths! Who the *hell* do you think you are, trying to. . .to manipulate me, patronise me, push me around?'

They faced each other, Charlotte's breathing jerky and irregular as she glowered at his impassive expression, then Drew grabbed her by the wrists and pulled her down on to the sofa beside him, forcing her round to meet his calculating appraisal.

'If you don't know who I am by now, I'll spell it out to you, as simply as I can! I'm the major shareholder in your father's boatyard. I'm a qualified naval architect, which means I can design and build whatever boats I choose to, *if* I choose to. I'm also the fortunate possessor of sufficient money to invest in Wells Boats. That money can either be used to revive the boat-building business, or used to develop the existing site into something even more profitable. . .'

She tried to wrench her wrists from his grasp, but

failed, and when she opened her mouth to retort he silenced her.

'Let me finish with a few home truths about your situation—you've just acted on sentimental impulse, abandoned your career for a bankrupt boatyard, with no capital, nowhere to live, and very little knowledge of the current boat-building market——'

'That's not true!' she blazed at him. 'I do know about boat-building. I'm not stupid!'

'Then prove it!' Drew snapped harshly. 'If you're not stupid, you'll accept any help you can get! Even from me!'

There was a hostile silence. Charlotte stared coldly at Drew, and the expression in his eyes reflected that coldness.

'All right.' She could barely form the words. 'Let go of my wrists, please.' The request was icily polite, and Drew released her abruptly, his eyes dropping to the red marks gradually forming on the pale skin.

'I'm sorry,' he said curtly. 'I didn't realise I was holding you so tightly. . .'

'Evidently.' She unbent sufficiently to rub her wrists, her eyes on the movement of her fingers. 'Maybe you don't know your own strength?' she suggested sarcastically, standing up. 'That's the second time tonight you've done that!'

Drew stood up too, looking paler suddenly beneath his habitual swarthiness. 'I apologise,' he repeated stiffly. 'I detest physical violence—for some reason I can't seem to keep my hands off you!'

'Maybe you could try a bit harder in future?' she suggested coolly. 'And don't be misled by appearances. I may look thin but I'm very strong. I may not compare with your sort of brawny strength, but my muscles are in very good working order!'

Drew's wide mouth twitched, but his expression stayed grave. 'I'm sure they are.' He narrowed his eyes, assessing her build, walking round her slowly. 'I think it's your narrow back that makes you look as if a gust of wind would blow you over. Very misleading.'

'Very. I'd like to get back to the flat now,' she said tightly, avoiding the glitter of laughter in his eyes. She was hanging on to her feelings so violently she felt as if a gust of wind would snap her in two at that moment.

'I can't persuade you to stay the night again?'

'No, thank you.'

The short drive back along the coast road was accomplished in malevolent silence. Drew accompanied her to the door of the basement flat, and insisted on seeing her safely inside before he left.

'I'll come and give you a hand with moving your things at the weekend. And don't worry about driving into the boatyard—I'll drive you.'

'I can manage, thank you. I do have my own transport.'

'That rusty old heap of Jonathan's?' He eyed the offending vehicle with a glint of amusement.

'My father's car is perfectly roadworthy. It's been

checked over by Paxtons only recently!' She was keeping a taut hold on her temper.

'Well, goodnight, then, Charlotte. Sleep well.'

'Goodnight!'

She thought she might bubble over with frustrated anger, and when he'd gone she slammed the door with a childish display of strength which went only a small way to alleviating her feelings.

'What you need,' Susie declared, eyeing Charlotte over the top of the box of books in her arms, 'is a holiday. Somewhere hot and sunny. You're looking so tense, darling! A week in the sun would do you a world of good.'

Charlotte paused in the act of hammering in a picture-hook, glancing over her shoulder with a disbelieving laugh. With a bushy pony-tail, workman's dungarees and a checked shirt, she looked like a tomboyish adolescent again.

'Some chance!' Charlotte's retort was brief.

'Why not?' Susie persisted, dumping the box of books and picking the top one off the pile curiously. 'I've just had a postcard from Antonia and Griff. They're sunning themselves again at her mother's place in Menorca. The temperatures are in the seventies, she says. I must say, she leads an enviably lazy existence! She always said she intended to be a lady of leisure, when we were at school. Remember?'

'Mmm. I expect she's bored stiff really. Too much money and not enough to do.' Charlotte carefully avoided Susie's eyes. The last thing she wanted to talk about was Antonia's jet-set lifestyle; it brought back too many unpleasant memories. 'And anyway, I'm not tense!' She turned back to the picture-hook, wielding the hammer with an unnecessary display of force. 'I just feel as if I could murder someone!'

'Well, I can't think why. If I'd been living in this exquisite cottage rent-free for a week, I'd feel more like hugging them to death!' Susie gestured around the low-ceilinged sitting-room, with its view of the wide river-mouth dotted with moored boats. 'Does Drew own all this land?'

Charlotte nodded resignedly, stepping back to appraise the position of the picture she'd just hung, a favourite scene of Shalmouth beach with a large ketch in the forefront. 'And a good stretch of the beach. So I can walk off my frustration every day in complete *safety* when I get home from work!'

'Women out walking on their own have been a target round here over the last six months. There have been a couple of assaults, in lonely "beauty spots". Peter keeps warning me not to go on my long country treks with the twins, but I detest the idea of being unable to go precisely where I please, when I please!' Susie glanced at Charlotte speculatively, adding, 'Maybe that's why your gorgeous Drew Meredith wants to keep you wrapped in cotton wool!'

'If only his motives were as pure!' Charlotte muttered bitterly.

'I suppose Drew pops in quite a lot, living just up the lane?' The enquiry was deceptively innocent.

'I haven't seen him since he gave me the keys last weekend.' She'd been both relieved and dismayed by his absence, but the dismayed part she wasn't about to admit to anyone.

'Has Fiona been here yet?'

'Yes, she was here a couple of days ago.'

'And?' Susie's tone was expectant, and Charlotte turned with a wry smile.

'She's hopping mad! She can't understand how Drew Meredith can possibly be so generous—and that makes two of us!'

'I'll bet she's also wishing you were on better terms, so that she could move in as well!' Susie laughed, not unkindly, flicking through the pages of Daphne Du Maurier's *Rebecca* as she extracted it from the box. 'Poor Fee. She's her own worst enemy!'

'How can you say that?' Charlotte was taken aback, her gaze fixed on the top of Susie's bent head. 'Fee's got everything going for her! She's. . .she's pretty, confident, attractive to men, successful in her career. . .'

'And a prize bitch as well!' Susie pronounced unrepentantly, ignoring Charlotte's disapproving gasp. 'She's mad keen on Drew Meredith—did you know? If I were you, I'd stake your claim there before things get decidedly tricky!'

Charlotte felt a wave of colour rising from her neck, and she turned her back on her friend, staring through the leaded window at the expanse of green-blue river, the water deceptively calm as the current ripped seawards beneath the surface. 'There's no claim to stake.'

'Who are you fooling? Drew Meredith may be a great philanthropist, given to random acts of generosity without any underlying motive, but I doubt it! You silly goose, why do you imagine he's let you have this cottage?'

'To salve his conscience!'

'Rubbish—anyway, why would he have to do that? He's agreed to let your trimaran deal go ahead, hasn't he?'

'At the moment. I'm not convinced he's serious about it. He'll do what he wants to, in the end. He's that kind of person. Anyway,' Charlotte switched the subject quickly, 'Fiona certainly wouldn't want to *live* in Cormorant Cottage. She likes ultra-modern, with everything brand-new and squeaky clean. She just objects to the principle of Drew handing out "largess" to me.'

'Mmm. She's jealous. I told you.'

'Well, there's certainly no need for her to be jealous of me!' Charlotte burst out, her emotions catching up on her unexpectedly, making her throat ache with unshed tears. 'This place was furnished and decorated by a female "friend" of Drew's, who's temporarily abroad! She's obviously Drew's current woman, and I've got the dubious pleasure of living in *her* house while she's away! Rest assured, Susie, there's nothing remotely romantic going on between

Drew and me. I'm really not the type of girl men go for. . .'

'That's not what Peter says,' Susie countered teasingly, eyeing her friend up and down with a knowledgeable air. 'He thinks you've got smouldering eyes, like Charlotte Rampling and Jacqueline Bisset!'

'Whereas in reality all she's got is a smouldering temper!' drawled Drew's deep voice from the doorway. Stomach plummeting, Charlotte swung round to see the familiar dark face creased in laughter, and she itched to pick up a book and throw it at him.

'Do you make a habit of sneaking up on people and eavesdropping on their conversations?' she enquired sweetly, ignoring Susie's dancing eyes. She wondered sinkingly how long he'd been there—had he heard her reference to the friend who'd decorated the cottage?

'I knocked,' Drew responded blithely, 'but no one answered. The door was open, so I came in.'

'Opportunist thieves probably have the same formula!'

'Probably. Anyway, I agree with Peter, whoever he is. You resemble Jacqueline Bisset to a marked degree.'

'My husband has good taste,' Susie chipped in, laughing as she prepared to leave. 'Look who he married! I'm Susie Helston,' she held out her hand expectantly to Drew, her brown eyes studying his impressive height and dark good looks approvingly, 'and, since Charlie obviously isn't going to introduce you, I'll hazard a guess that you're Drew Meredith?'

'Correct.' Charlotte watched Drew's long eyes crinkle at the corners as he took Susie's hand and smiled, thinking with a pang how charming Drew could be when he tried.

'I'll see you later, Charlie, darling,' Susie was saying cheerfully. 'I'd better get back to the terrible twins, but you will come and have tea with them tonight, won't you?'

'Of course I will—I'll babysit as well, if you want. If Peter's not at Heathrow this weekend?' Susie's husband was a pilot, frequently away on long-haul flights, so his spells at home were too precious to waste.

'No, he's got a couple of days' leave. Would you really babysit? I hate inflicting the twins on people I don't know very well—they're such a liability!'

'I'll babysit with pleasure. And there's no need to rush off now, Susie. . .' The pleading note was audible even to Charlotte's own ears, and she bit her lip, annoyed with herself. She could handle Drew on her own, she didn't have to reveal how nervous she felt in his company.

'Settled in?' he asked smoothly, when Susie's car had disappeared from view.

'As you can see.'

Drew glanced around the room, eyeing her personal touches with cool interest. She watched him reluctantly. The close-fitting black cords and loose black sweatshirt he wore emphasised his dark colouring, accentuated the loose-limbed power of his body. She found herself thinking about the kiss, in the car. Her stomach was doing acrobatics as she waited for him to say something else.

Drew was examining her collection of antique tiles, hung plate-style on the wall above the fireplace.

'I hope you don't mind my hanging things on the walls. . .?' She wondered belatedly if she should have asked his permission first.

'Not at all. These are unusual. . .'

'Some are Minton—most of them are Victorian,' she explained. 'They're not valuable.'

'You're an authority on this kind of thing?'

'Not really, no. . .'

'But you obviously collect them?'

'It's just a sort of hobby—it started when some Minton black and white tiles fetched a few hundred pounds at the auction house. They caught my interest, I suppose. I hadn't realised there was a market in antique tiles! Afterwards I came across a little junk shop in London where they sold old tiles for a few pounds each. Then I got hooked, hunting round the antique shops for bargains. . .'

'Do you miss your job in London?'

'In some ways. . .but there are antique shops in Devon. . .' She felt on the defensive immediately. Was he trying to edge her out of Wells Boats by reminding her of the career she'd abandoned?

Drew seemed preoccupied, reaching down into

the box of books and inspecting a battered edition of *Heidi* with a deadpan expression.

Charlotte fidgeted uncomfortably in the ensuing silence. 'Was there something you wanted?' she enquired at last, beginning to feel strangely vulnerable to Drew's calm investigation of her possessions.

'Mrs Bolton intends to come in and clean and iron twice a week,' he said at last, putting the book back, and noting the rebellious set of her soft mouth without a flicker. 'She won't take no for an answer, I'm afraid. She's always looked on Cormorant Cottage as part of her territory.'

'Doesn't she find the ghosts off-putting?'

'She's all right as long as it's daylight.' Drew's lips quirked slightly at her innocent expression.

'Well, I'd hate to tread on Mrs Bolton's toes. Is that all you came to say?'

'No, I came to ask you to crew for me tomorrow. I'm delivering a sloop up to the Hamble.'

'Why do you need me? You employ dozens of skippers, don't you?'

'I'd like you to come,' he said shortly. 'We can combine business with pleasure.'

'In what way?'

'We can talk about Greg's trimaran—he's coming along as well.'

'Oh! Well, in that case. . .' she said, with more enthusiasm. Drew was the last person she would confess it to, but Greg Smithson had proved a difficult man to pin down over the last week. Maybe Drew's casual one-month deadline was making her

over-anxious, making her try too hard. . .but if
Drew had met Greg, and was inviting him sailing
with them, that relieved two major worries. Greg
wasn't about to pull out, and Drew must be intending to honour his word over the fate of Wells Boats,
mustn't he?

'Of course I'll come,' she finished up, with a smile.

'For the business or the pleasure?' Drew asked,
noting her more cheerful expression with what
looked like grim irony.

'What's that supposed to mean?'

'Only that when I bumped into Greg Smithson in
the Beach Inn the other night he spoke glowingly of
you. I gathered he was another of your
"conquests"?'

She flushed scarlet. 'Don't be so ridiculous,' she
said shortly. 'I don't make "conquests"! Greg's a
business contact.'

'So you've bowled him over with your business
acumen?' Drew sounded bleakly amused. 'I have to
admit I was impressed by what he said—considering
you're an inexperienced girl of twenty-three you've
certainly convinced Greg Smithson that Wells Boats
can give him what he wants!'

'And we can.' She chose to ignore the subtle
ambiguity of Drew's remark. She'd had enough of
his warped mind—from now on she would pretend
she hadn't heard.

She stood her ground, eyeing him levelly, hands
thrust firmly in the pockets of her dungarees, her
chin thrust upwards in unconscious challenge. Drew

stared down at her for a few moments, his hard features shadowed and unreadable.

'Yes, Charlie. I think we probably can.'

Without warning, he bent his head and kissed her briefly and soundly on the lips, then withdrew a fraction, his eyes narrowed on her face. She looked up into his eyes, and the heat she encountered took her so much by surprise her lips parted on a quick in-breath, and Drew bent to kiss her again, in a way that disturbed her so deeply she clutched at his upper-arms to support herself. There seemed no value in protesting when he moved his arms around her, enfolding her securely against him while he deepened the kiss, stringing out the simple physical action into such a lingering affair she began to drown in unbearable, languorous pleasure.

Even his look of calm triumph when he eventually disengaged himself and held her a few inches away from him failed to arouse her previous antagonism. She stared at him, shakily, willing the quivering curiosity inside her to drift away again as insidiously as it had come. Kisses like that were like an illicit draught of champagne. This one had left her with the bewildered sensation that her carefully positioned defences were about as effective as the house of straw against the wolf.

'Your immune system seems to be as erratic as ever, Charlie.'

She couldn't deny it. She just stood there, staring at him idiotically.

'I'll call for you in the morning. Half-past six. That's not too early for you, I hope?'

'No,' she said huskily, shaking her head. She wasn't sleeping too well these nights. She was normally awake long before that. And she had the premonition that this particular night was going to be the worst so far.

The tides and the winds would be with them most of the way, Drew announced as they left Shalmouth early the next morning. Charlotte felt ridiculously happy as she clambered about the thirty-foot sloop, the icy wind stinging her cheeks as it filled the jib and mainsail with satisfying force. Surprisingly, she'd slept quite well the night before—not even Mrs Bolton's ghosts had disturbed her—until five o'clock, when she'd woken and lain there in a sleepy half-doze, reliving the feel of Drew's mouth on hers.

She was probably being naïve, but to her mind there'd been a gentleness, a tenderness in the way Drew had kissed her, a quality that hadn't been there before. Her spirits seemed to draw strength from this notion, like a plant seeking water, and even the memory of past wrongs, even the thought of the mysterious female interior decorator lurking somewhere abroad, couldn't disperse her stubborn euphoria.

She could hardly credit herself with feeling the way she did. Only a short time ago, she'd been wishing Drew Meredith somewhere very unpleasant indeed. How come she was seeing him in a different light all of a sudden? Was she really as fickle as Drew seemed to think?

She wound the jib sheet vigorously and looped it around the cleat to bring the sails into a perfect close-hauled setting, conscious of Drew's shrewd appraisal as he climbed past her to throw the jib sail-bag into the locker.

'It's blowing Force Five,' he said, eyeing the wind indicator above the cabin entrance, and glancing approvingly at the set of the sails. 'We should go like a train today.'

Greg grinned at them from his position at the helm, blue eyes twinkling. He was several years younger than Drew, probably late twenties, and exuded a boyish enthusiasm Charlotte found quite endearing.

'Fantastic. I've spent too much time at the draw-ing-board recently, not enough out on the water! This little sloop handles like a dream, Drew!'

'Yes, I'm quite pleased with the design, you can turn her on a sixpence,' Drew said conversationally, squinting at the echo-sounder and ducking below to consult the navigation charts. 'Take her across to starboard, Greg, we're too near the sandbank.'

'You designed this sloop?' Charlotte felt embar-rassed displaying so little knowledge about her 'part-ner', but curiosity got the better of her.

'Yes. Shalmouth Sea School operates quite a fleet of these.'

'Who builds them?'

'There's a huge factory near Southampton that

churns them out on a production line,' Drew told her casually, reading her mind. 'And no, Wells Boats could not take over the business. Not in its present premises, anyway! Wells's future may lie in small, specialist projects, like Greg's trimaran—it certainly doesn't lie in mass production!'

She could see the justice of this, and said nothing. She obviously still knew very little about Drew, she thought crossly. For years, she'd just thought of him as a sailor who ran his own skipper business. The possibility of his being involved in all aspects of the marine business hadn't occurred to her. She hadn't known he was a naval architect, and she hadn't realised he designed his own boats for his sea school. Drew was right, she thought miserably, she was inexperienced, naïve, signally lacking in knowledge of the ways of the business world.

When she came to consider it, it was obvious he was a very rich man. The manor house by the estuary, in all its glorious acres, didn't come cheap. Wells Boats must seem like a very small fish indeed to Drew Meredith. Her father must have left him all those shares to ensure some money, at least, would be available to bail out the business. And he would have known, too, how well qualified Drew was to take over the yard.

'You're very pensive, Charlotte.' Greg was smiling at her, as she sat in the cockpit, staring at the jagged coastline receding into the distance. 'I'm really sorry about your father. It must have been a shock.'

'Yes. . .it was. My life seems to have turned upside-down in the last few weeks. . .' She was momentarily surprised how hard it still was to respond to well-meaning words of sympathy. But it had only been a matter of weeks since Dad died. . .it seemed longer, much longer. So much had happened, she'd been under such emotional attack from other quarters, there'd hardly been time to mourn, to come to terms with her loss. . .Greg's kindness uncovered the gaping hole of grief inside her, and she turned away quickly, blocking out the pain.

'Drew tells me your mother's dead too. That's really tough. If you want a shoulder to cry on, you know where to come.'

'Thanks, Greg. I'll bear that in mind!' She laughed lightly in return.

'Let's make a firm date, in fact. Have dinner with me one night this week?'

'Well. . .' She bit her lip, very aware out of the corner of her eye that Drew was watching and listening to this brief exchange. There was very little you could discuss privately on a boat. Drew's expression, when she met his eyes, was coldly sardonic, and her heart contracted. Critical, judgemental, that summed him up. What an impossibly cynical man he was, she decided bitterly. Small wonder his marriage had foundered if he read innuendo into every innocent conversation between male and female. What was she supposed to do? Be downright unfriendly, risk losing her trimaran order? Maybe that would suit Drew perfectly, said a small, suspicious voice at the back of her mind.

'Thanks, Greg. I'd love to,' she said firmly, deeply resenting that censorious look.

'Great! What's your favourite food? French? Japanese? Italian?'

'Slow down, Shalmouth isn't London, you know!'

'She likes Spanish food, French wine, and black coffee,' Drew drawled over his shoulder, his laconic tone not matching the ice in his glance.

Greg looked slightly startled. Charlotte simmered with indignation. How dared Drew talk about her as if she were a pet cat being handed over to another owner?

'Your information's out of date, I'm afraid,' she lied lightly, 'I much prefer Chinese to Spanish now. Funny how tastes change with maturity.'

Greg beamed. 'Chinese is my favourite too. Chinese it is, then. I've the feeling you and I are going to have lots in common, Charlotte!'

She winced inwardly at this declaration, and a profound silence followed, broken only by the creak of the sails in the wind. Drew had turned his back on her, his broad shoulders ominously set.

'This is so exhilarating!' she said, desperately switching the subject away from the personal. 'I'd forgotten how good it is to sail! Do you mind if I take the helm?'

'Feel free. . .' Greg moved aside and she took the tiller, feeling the boat respond under her fingers. Greg sat close beside her in the cockpit, and began relating his life story, while Charlotte kept one eye on the automatic compass and the other on Drew's unyielding back, as he leaned inside the entrance leading down into the cabin, gazing silently out to sea.

'So you're not a naval architect?' she queried, as he explained how he'd come to design his trimaran. 'Just an ordinary architect?'

'The disciplines are similar,' Greg said, smiling so admiringly into her eyes she began to wonder what on earth he could find attractive in her appearance. Layers of thermal underwear, jeans and sweatshirts, topped by padded oilskin salopettes, anorak and a woolly hat were not exactly the ultimate in sexual allure. 'Once you've learned how to design buildings, you can apply some of that knowledge to designing a boat. All you have to do is decide what you want the hull to do—then gauge from that what shape it needs to be to do that job correctly. Wouldn't you say that's so, Drew?'

'Sounds logical. There's bound to be a parallel in the methodology.' Drew glanced over his shoulder, his eyes narrowed to a thoughtful squint into the pale sunshine. 'The main problem with designing racing yachts tends to be the balance between speed and safety.'

Greg grinned confidently, apparently immune to the dry sarcasm Charlotte detected in Drew's tone. 'Yeah, sure. But the Westwind attracts some pretty fast customers! To win the forty-foot class you've got to be faster!'

'How long have you been sailing?'

'Three years!' Greg announced proudly, laughing at Charlotte's surprise. 'I know it's not long. But I'm hooked, well and truly. My family think I'm mental! I've run up a monumental overdraft, borrowed money from my parents, practically pawned everything I can lay my hands on, to get this project rolling.'

'Brave man,' Drew murmured, his tone unmoved. Charlotte looked up at him sharply, but his expression was as deadpan as his tone.

'Well, nothing ventured, nothing gained!' Greg said cheerfully.

'Or alternatively, fools step in. . .?' Drew had turned his back on them again, ducking back down to the navigation desk to check their course. Charlotte wanted to hit Drew. This was supposed to be a public relations outing, wasn't it? To encourage Greg Smithson, not dampen his enthusiasm?

Drew's forecast of tides and winds was correct. The trip was completed in thirteen hours, record time, but what had begun as exhilarating finished up cold and exhausting, and she was secretly glad to motor up the Hamble river in the darkness and moor on a pontoon within walking distance of a hotel. She hadn't enquired about the sleeping arrangements, but, while she'd brought her sleeping-bag as a matter of course, the usual procedure of sleeping on board the boat failed to appeal, tonight. For one thing, today's trip had coincided with an awkward time in her monthly cycle, and in any case sailing around the English coast in early spring was a decidedly masochistic occupation, a fact she'd conveniently forgotten during her spell of exile in London.

Her spirits cheered, however, when the hotel boasted a blazing log fire and a management receptive to Drew's polite but authoritative demands for a late meal.

'You're glowing tonight!' Greg told her fulsomely, as she chose the table in the bar nearest the fire. He was openly appraising her sparkling green eyes and rosy cheeks, his gaze roving boldly over her willowy figure in blue denims and white sweatshirt, minus the bulky cladding of foul-weather gear. 'You look as if you've been taken out of deep freeze and thawed back to life! Would you like me to chafe your fingers and toes, or would you like a drink, Charlotte?'

'Scotch, please, Greg. I may take you up on the other offer later, if the fire doesn't revive my toes!' She laughed at Greg, shaking back her cloudy dark curls, a pleasant wave of physical tiredness relaxing her as she leaned back in her seat. The icy wind out at sea had left her tingling all over at the sudden contrast in temperature, and, in spite of her reservations about the weather, she felt the curious contented satisfaction that only a long, challenging sail could produce.

But a glance in Drew's direction rapidly dissipated the contentment. His expression was bleak, and his cool silence as Greg hurried off to the bar made her aware of him in every nerve of her body. Tension crept back, and she felt a wave of angry resentment at his ability to affect her mood.

'Has he signed anything yet?' Drew's voice was laconic, and she looked at him warily.

'What do you mean?'

'Has Greg Smithson signed a contract for Wells Boats to build his trimaran?'

'Well, no. . .he hasn't actually put pen to paper. But he's bound to soon—the race he's entering for is in August, so we'd be hard pushed to finish it if we don't get started pretty quickly. . .'

'Have you seen his plans?'

'Of course!' She sat up straighter, glancing round at the crowded bar. Greg's sandy head could be seen in a substantial queue for drinks. 'They look good, Drew. Exciting—he's put a lot of original thought into his design, made sure the cockpit area is very streamlined, for instance, to avoid bumps and bruises and all the usual discomfort, and he's brought all the lines back into the cockpit so one person can sail the boat really easily. . .'

Drew nodded slowly, his dark face unreadable. When he remained silent, she felt like shaking him.

'What's the problem? What are you driving at?' she asked at last, her voice taut. 'I've noticed you've been singularly lacking in enthusiasm all day—is this where you stop humouring me and decide to pull rank after all? Was the purpose of today's outing to subtly get rid of Greg Smithson and leave the way clear for your bulldozers?'

Drew was inscrutable. 'Stop being paranoid.'

'Then why this interrogation? And why are you being so bloody-minded today? Yesterday I thought——' She stopped abruptly, reddening as the lazy amber stare focused more intently on her face.

'Go on. What did you think yesterday, Charlie?' His tone was soft, but far from gentle.

'It doesn't matter.' Greg was approaching, a tray of drinks in his hands, and she greeted him with rather more warmth than necessary, her anger awakening a reckless urge to enjoy Greg's cheerful undemanding company in spite of Drew's implacable mood.

'We'll stay the night here, if you like,' Drew suggested casually, as they studied the menu. 'Unless you're keen to freeze on board the boat, or hire a car and drive back tonight?'

Charlotte had indeed assumed that if they stayed anywhere, it would be on board the boat. Her sleeping-bag was stowed away in the forepeak cabin for just such an eventuality. But Drew was looking at Greg as he spoke, and the younger man shrugged good-humouredly.

'Fine by me. I'll go and check the tariff, shall I. . .?' Greg made to stand up but Drew rose instead, with a brief shake of the head.

'Forget it—since the sloop I designed doesn't boast central heating, Shalmouth Sea School can foot the bill.' He disappeared into the reception area, and returned after a short space of time with three room keys.

They settled down in relative good humour to
choose a meal from the restaurant menu. But not
even a delicious steak, and two bottles of vintage
burgundy in the welcoming atmosphere of the
dining-room, seemed to mellow Drew. The sailing
talk flowed as easily as the wine, but the underlying
thread of unease lingered, a whiff of menace beneath
the superficial socialising.

Charlotte kept up a vivacious conversation with
Greg, deliberately encouraging him to talk about his
family in Somerset, his parents and his brother and
two sisters. She learned that his father was a bank
manager, his mother a teacher. As they drank more
wine, the talk became more personal, and Greg
grew more brazen in his light-hearted line in flirtation. He'd been engaged for a while, he informed
her soulfully, but had broken it off when he'd
realised his fiancée would never share his love of
sailing. What he'd been searching for all along, he
declared, was a girl like Charlie. Someone who could
enjoy moving in a man's world yet retain her
femininity.

Charlotte raised a teasing eyebrow, hardly daring
to look at Drew. But when she did, his sardonic
mockery brought a hectic flush to her cheeks. With
a sudden unwelcome flood of memory, she felt as if
they were re-enacting a part, a replay of the dramas
of Menorca, only this time she recognised her behaviour with Greg was subconsciously deliberate, she
was being goaded into flirting with another man. . .

She stood up, suddenly exhausted. She could

hardly keep her eyes open, her stomach hurt, and she couldn't wait to collapse into a comfortable hotel bed.

'Sorry, I'm too tired to stay awake any longer,' she declared apologetically. 'I'll have to go to bed.' She lifted her arms and yawned hugely.

'Need any help undressing?' Greg's eyes were lingering on the outline of her breasts through the soft material of her sweatshirt, as she stretched.

'Give me your room number,' she joked, 'then if I need anything unhooking I'll know where to come!'

Drew grated back his chair, the look in his eyes so menacing that Charlotte's heart began to thud painfully against her ribs. For an agonising moment she thought Drew was going to hit Greg, but he seemed to have his physical reactions under iron control. Besides, a voice enquired in her head, what possible reason would Drew have for attacking Greg Smithson? Jealousy? But people were only jealous if they cared about someone deeply, and that certainly wasn't the situation between Drew and herself. . .

'I'll go and get your rucksack from the boat.' Drew's voice was harsh with suppressed anger, abrasive after Greg's good-natured banter.

'Please don't bother. . .' She had her shoulder-bag with the necessary feminine requisites, and she slung it firmly over her shoulder. 'I can't stay awake long enough to wait for it. . .' she began, but the steely determination in Drew's face made her stop.

'Go up to your room,' he said abruptly, handing her a key, for all the world like an autocratic headmaster about to administer a lecture in morality. 'I'll bring your gear up to you.'

'Drew, really, there's no need. . .' she started to say, as politely as she could. She was acutely aware of Greg's interested presence. At all costs she must avoid an unbusinesslike row with Drew in front of such a valuable customer. Apart from anything else, Drew's arrogant display of bossiness was too humiliating.

'There's every need,' he countered, with a cold smile which came nowhere near his eyes. 'We can't have you cleaning your teeth with your finger.'

Her answering smile was a matching parody of his, as she nodded a brief goodnight to Greg, her face burning.

'Goodnight. . .see you in the morning, Greg,' she managed to say, with commendable composure, before making a stiffly dignified journey up to her room to wait, furiously, for the delivery of her rucksack.

CHAPTER SEVEN

Too angry to do anything but pace around the room, Charlotte moved restlessly to the window, drawing the curtains against the darkness, then marched to the *en suite* bathroom, securely locking the door even though her room door was also locked, washing her face and hands with a ferocity which banished all traces of sleepiness.

When she heard Drew's knock, she flung open the door and faced him furiously.

'What the *hell* do you think you're playing at?' she burst out, taking the rucksack and hurling it down on the floor. Without preamble, Drew pushed his way past her, and slammed the door behind him, the ruthless glitter in his eyes almost matching the fiery challenge in hers.

'I was about to ask you the same thing!' His clipped fury was like a razor blade slashing at her emotions, and she stepped back involuntarily, tripped over the end of the bed and found herself sitting down inelegantly, her legs sprawled in front of her. 'Our friend Greg Smithson seems to think he's in with a fighting chance of "getting to first base" with you! Do you have to act like a bitch in heat whenever you get within a yard of the opposite sex?'

She was off the bed like a wildcat, fists clenched, green eyes spitting fire.

'You're *pathetic*!' she choked, struggling for breath. 'With your *cynical* mind, and your *warped* imagination——' words failed her for a few moments, and she grappled to articulate her hostility '—you wouldn't recognise a normal emotion if it hit you in the face! Get out! Get out!'

'Since I'm paying for the room, I'll go when I'm ready to go. I thought I'd just let you know you can forget about your prospective new lover—he's opted for the quiet life. Sorry to disappoint you, Charlie. . .'

She stared at him in stormy silence, trying to grasp what he was telling her. Visions of Greg withdrawing from the trimaran deal, seeking another boat-builder, flashed into her mind. Then an even more gruesome scenario. . .had he had a *fight* with Greg, after all? Surely Drew wouldn't stoop to such barbaric behaviour? She didn't know. She didn't know him any more. It was doubtful if she ever had. A split-second comparison between Drew's supple, loose-limbed physique, accentuated by the close-fitting denims and heavy guernsey, and Greg's slighter build, made such a nightmare seem only too possible. She let out a sob of pure frustration. 'What have you done, Drew?'

'It's all right. . .' his laugh was coldly mocking. '. . .I told you I detest violence. I haven't shot him in the kneecaps or shaved his head!'

'But you've ruined the trimaran deal, haven't you?

You supercilious *bastard*! How dare you barge in here as if you owned me. . .?' She flew at him, beside herself with rage, kicking and punching, meeting an iron-hard wall of muscle wherever the blows fell, until abruptly Drew's rigid restraint deserted him and she was jerked into stillness by a grip which knocked the breath out of her.

'Maybe that's what's torturing me. . .lack of ownership?' he mocked harshly, pinning her against him to stop her struggles. 'I'm not proud of myself, Charlie! Hell knows, I need you like I need a dose of poison, but it doesn't help. . .nothing helps. . .' The last was ground despairingly against her hair, his mouth brutally covering her muffled protests, forcing her cries back into her throat as he half lifted, half pushed her on to the bed.

A few moments earlier, she'd fooled herself that her display of fierce strength could be a match for Drew, but that notion was quickly disproved. Drew's sustained assault on her senses had all the bravura of a pirate, and what started out as a ferocious tussle switched without warning to a feverish, shuddering meeting of lips and tongues and bodies, the heavy silence broken only by her shaken gasps of surprise at the swelling tumult of emotion inside her. Her brain reeled in confusion as his hands began to peel the white sweatshirt upwards, his long fingers expertly feeling for fasteners and straps among the layers of clothing. Fear and anger became inextricably mixed with such piercingly urgent longings Charlotte felt dizzy with bewilderment. The sweatshirt was removed in spite of her protests, and with shaking hands Drew slid down several extremely unromantic layers of thermal underwear to expose her aching breasts to his view.

'Drew, please don't. . .' She lifted her hands helplessly, to ward him off, but her words choked in her throat as his dark head bent down to her breasts, and his cool lips moved across the tightly clenched peak of each nipple, sucking and licking until she convulsed beneath him, clutching his head and weaving her fingers into the thickness of his black hair, her eyes wide with disbelief at the sensations his hands and mouth could unleash in her.

Everything became a blur of heat and touch and taste, her senses aroused to such a pitch it wasn't until he sought to undress her further that reality came crashing back. She couldn't let Drew make love to her—not now, in anger and bitterness and suspicion, and not anyway, not tonight. . .

'No!' she burst out, finding strength to fight again as he slid down the zip of her jeans. 'Stop it!'

'Not this time, Charlie. You want me as much as I want you.' The deep, husky voice sent arrows of desire streaking through her groin.

'No!'

'Let me undress you, Charlie. . .' He was tearing at his own clothes impatiently, flinging them haphazardly to the floor, and she stared in choked wonder at the miraculous width of dark, silken skin, at the black hair on chest and forearms, the V of dark hair pointing down the rock-flat stomach to the fastening of his jeans. She was shaking violently, she realised, clutching her arms around herself, and she could see that Drew, too, was trembling slightly as he looked down at her.

'Charlie. . .'

'No! I can't. . .it's not possible. . .' She bit her lip, miserably aware how ambiguous her protests sounded, hot with embarrassment as Drew's amber gaze raked down over her semi-nakedness, the fire in their depths leaving her in no doubt about his intentions, and a wave of alarm pulsed through her.

'Feel what you do to me. . .' he ordered harshly, grabbing her hand and laying it against him, watching the wild colour flare in her cheeks as she traced the rearing hardness of him beneath the rough denim. 'I've waited long enough! You're driving me insane!'

'Drew, don't! Just leave me alone, please. . . don't' His hands were caressing the long, slender expanse of her thighs, his probing fingers becoming more insistent, more tantalising, and with a frantic sob she curled over on her side, pulling her knees up and hugging herself protectively, terrified at the intense excitement he was generating in her with the impulsive heat of his lovemaking. 'Please, Drew! Even if I wanted to go any further, I'm. . . I'm indisposed!' she burst out, in a strangled voice.

'What?'

'It's the wrong time of the *month*!'

There was a long moment of tense silence, as Drew's demanding hands stilled on her body, and then with her eyes squeezed tight shut she heard him curse softly under his breath. She could almost feel the sexual tension draining from the atmosphere. Did she imagine a trace of rueful *laughter* in his tone when he spoke at last?

'Charlie, I'm sorry!'

She couldn't move, she was rigid with embarrassment, and resentment. Did he really find this situation amusing? Well, if he had a warped mind, presumably he had a warped sense of humour to go with it.

After a while he gathered her gently against him, and she found her face against the hard muscle of his chest. He threaded his fingers into her tangled hair, shakily stroking her head.

'I'm sorry. . .oh, hell. . .' His deep voice was still thick with emotion, and she shivered, twisting out of his arms, appalled at the unbearable intimacy of the situation. Jerking her sweatshirt over her head, she made a bolt for the bathroom, where she splashed cold water over her swollen face and bleakly blew her nose.

Drew was standing at the window when she came out. He'd opened the top sash of the window and had lit a cigar, and he seemed to be deeply preoccupied by his thoughts.

She stopped abruptly as she caught sight of him, unable to prevent herself from staring at the wonderful expanse of darkly tanned torso above strong, denim-clad legs. He had the supple, athletic build of a sportsman. She was mesmerised by the long, hard back, the aura of relaxed power he managed to radiate without even moving a muscle.

Sensing her presence, he turned, and her throat dried up again as the muscles moved and rippled. Was she unnatural? she wondered frantically. Was it normal to find one particular man so physically attractive that she was temporarily robbed of the powers of speech?

'Do you mind?' he asked, his expression unreadable. A pulse was throbbing in his temple, she noticed absently, and she recognised that far from finding the situation amusing Drew was feeling just as tense as she was. 'Smoking in someone else's bedroom is out of order. But in the absence of a cold shower, I felt I needed this.'

'You should give it up. It's bad for you,' she said coolly, walking over to the bed and sitting self-consciously on the edge, taking a ruthless grip on her wayward hormones. With a wry grimace, Drew stubbed the cigar out in the ashtray on the dressing-table, and came over to the bed.

She couldn't bring herself to look at him. 'I want you to go now, Drew. I'm tired. . .'

'Charlotte, we have to talk——'

'Not tonight. I don't feel like talking now.'

He squatted down easily in front of her, putting his hands gently on her shoulders. 'Look at me, Charlotte.'

She stared resolutely down at her clasped hands in her lap, and Drew slid his hand along the side of her neck, tilting her chin up with his thumb.

'Charlotte, what happened just now is something I should be ashamed of, not you,' he said grimly. 'So will you stop avoiding my eyes?'

'Put your shirt on, then!' she said tersely, trembling inside at his touch, and at the sudden kindling of understanding in his eyes. Straightening with athletic ease, he picked up the discarded item and shrugged it on, watching her levelly as he fastened a few of the buttons. She found she couldn't drag her eyes away as he tucked the soft, beige checked cotton into his denims.

'Better?' His amber eyes were gleaming wryly, and she nodded abruptly.

He searched her white face, coming to sit beside her on the bed. The emotional tension of the past few minutes had sent her stomach into painful cramps, and she gritted her teeth as another cramp speared through her.

'You look pale. Are you all right? Can I get you something?'

'I'm not ill,' she said shortly, evading his eyes again. 'There's nothing wrong a couple of stiff gins wouldn't cure! And I wish you'd just go away!'

Drew leaned over to the telephone by her bed, and waited implacably for the receptionist to answer. 'Send a bottle of gin up to Room Eight, will you, please?'

Charlotte put her hands to her face, feeling overpowered by Drew's obstinate taking charge of the situation. 'For heaven's sake, I was *joking*!' she protested hotly. 'What on earth will that receptionist think of me?'

'She'll write you off as a dipsomaniac.'

'An unmarried dipsomaniac with a man in her bedroom.'

'I'll tell her you're my fiancée if it makes you feel better?'

'That won't be necessary, thank you.'

Drew suddenly raked his hand impatiently through his tousled hair, his voice deepening. 'Charlotte. . .' She swallowed convulsively at the darkening of his eyes as he held her gaze. 'I was in a black rage just now—I've been in some rages before but, so help me, I've never tried to *force* a woman——' He stopped, rubbing his fingers across his forehead wearily. 'I've behaved badly,' he finished up, with a grim laugh. 'Whenever I'm with you, I behave badly!'

'Why?' She felt compelled to ask, her heart beginning to pound in her chest. She ought to agree with him, tell him to go to hell, but her emotions felt shredded. Tonight's happenings had left her shaky and vulnerable, and, besides, she had the uncomfortable feeling that this confession worked both ways. She couldn't claim to be a paragon of perfection either, when it came to Drew Meredith. . .'When. . .when you kissed me yesterday, at the cottage. . .' she bit her lip, forcing herself to go on '. . .I began to feel you actually *liked* me, instead of *despising* me!'

Drew closed his eyes for a few moments, and

when he opened them again the pupils seemed to have enlarged, darkening the golden irises. He searched her face intently, and she felt mesmerised. 'Despise you? I've never despised you.'

'You have! In the past you've accused me of throwing myself at you, then jumping into bed with another man! And tonight proved nothing's changed! You came barging in here, calling me names! You think the worst of me, no matter what the situation!'

Drew was motionless for a while, then he slowly straightened up and walked over to the window, where the yellow cotton curtains were billowing out like sails in the breeze. This time the silence stretched on so long, she began to think he'd never break it.

'I met a girl when I was eighteen,' he said at last, conversational rather than confiding. 'She was only seventeen. It was one of those impulsive "young love" affairs everyone sneers at. But I was a romantic youth, God help me. I was on leave from the Navy, and I was searching for something I'd never managed to find up till then. . .someone who could "belong" to me, and to no one else, I suppose. I'm not sure. . .but I was naïve enough to believe when she swore undying love for me, that was what she meant.' He glanced over his shoulder, his expression shadowed with self-mockery. 'To cut a long story short, she got pregnant, and to stop her from having an abortion I married her. The rest is a bit sordid. The baby turned out to be non-existent, and the "marriage" couldn't survive separations while I went off on Naval exercises. I came home on leave and found her in bed with my closest friend. . .'

'Oh, Drew——'

'This is ancient history,' he said smoothly, cutting across her murmur of distress. 'He was friend enough to tell me she hadn't singled only him out for her favours—it seemed that Debbie had slept with half the crew of a nuclear submarine in my absence. For some reason he thought that made it better. . .'

'Drew——'

'Anyway, to sum up, I divorced Debbie, I spent four more years in the Navy, then I took a degree course at the UCL, and then I came to Shalmouth, and made the acquaintance of my real father, who transpired to be the shallowest, most self-centred womaniser I'd ever met.' He turned back to hold her eyes levelly, his gaze bleak. 'I told you I'm no good at explaining my feelings. What I'm trying to say is, it's taken me years to learn not to think the worst of people. It wasn't until relatively recently I worked out why people behave badly, Charlie. But there's usually a reason. Loneliness, insecurity. . .usually they're looking for some romantic version of love. The more they've been deprived of it, the more they seek it. . .searching for something that doesn't exist. . .'

She felt sick suddenly, as his meaning sank in. She hadn't realised how much she'd been secretly hoping Drew might return her feelings. She hadn't even identified her true feelings, underneath the jumble of resentment and anger. His cool dismissal of love should have been exactly what she expected from him, but instead it came as a brutal blow, exposing her own foolishness. Charlotte stood up abruptly, trying to control her childish urge to burst into tears again.

'Like me, you mean? That poor, deluded little seventeen-year-old who hero-worshipped you, and was too dense to read the "keep off" signs? What are you trying to do to me, telling me all this?' she demanded flatly. 'Bore me to sleep? What's all this "ancient history" got to do with what's been going on today?'

Something flickered abruptly in Drew's eyes, but there was a knock on the door before he could reply, and he went to answer it. A bland-faced waitress stood there with the ordered gin, complete with tonic and two glasses. Drew gave her a generous tip, and she smiled at him, her curious eyes looking past him to where Charlotte stood, arms clutched round herself in acute misery, and she could imagine the girl retreating downstairs to share the latest gossip with the rest of the night staff.

'At the risk of mixing grape and grain, drink that, Charlotte.' She was steered firmly on to the bed, and the glass pushed into her hand. Drew's concerned expression was a fair indicator of how ghastly she must look.

'I'm perfectly OK,' she told him sharply, taking a reckless swig of the neat spirit to drown her misery, and feeling it burn fierily all the way down to her stomach. 'Ugh! I can't stand gin!'

She gulped some more, feeling the heat spreading right through her limbs, making her slightly light-headed.

'I can't win tonight, can I?' Drew's tone was dry. 'Go easy on that stuff——'

'Why?' she demanded, her green eyes glittering. 'You're the one who insisted I have it! And you're the one who thinks alcohol's a multi-purpose cure-all—grief, shock, heartache, period pain—just bring out the whisky or the gin!' She was getting slightly tight, and a fraction hysterical, and she knew it, but the dammed-up pain in her was too much to hold in any longer. If Drew could behave badly, so could she!

'Charlie——'

'Gin always depresses me,' she declared suddenly, inconsequently, tears spilling over, running unchecked down her face.

'Don't drink any more, then,' Drew suggested patiently, his expression grim as he twisted the cap firmly back on the bottle, and took it over to the dressing-table. 'I don't want a case of alcohol poisoning on my conscience!'

He came back to her, and bent over her, his eyes shadowed with regret. 'Get yourself to bed, Charlotte. You're exhausted. Thirteen hours' sailing can knock anyone out——'

'So can almost getting raped!'

He'd reached the door when she blurted it out,

and he stopped short, turning to look searchingly into her face, his expression taut with pain.

'Is that how it felt, Charlotte? Am I really so. . .distasteful to you now?' His voice had deepened and roughened.

She bit her lip, grabbing for a tissue to blow her nose. 'Yes!' she lied passionately, rounding on him. 'Yes, you are! Bloody distasteful! So go away and leave me alone!'

'Charlie!' Drew sounded torn apart.

'Oh, just go away!' she sobbed. 'Please, Drew! Just leave me alone!'

'Goodnight, Charlotte.' The dark face was shuttered as he turned away, and the door closed quietly behind him. Charlotte slammed the glass down on the bedside table, and buried her face in her hands.

The next two weeks were the worst Charlotte could ever remember. To stop herself thinking about Drew, she immersed herself totally in the boatyard's affairs, slept badly, and worried constantly. Since the cool, subdued breakfast, and tense drive back to Shalmouth, she'd heard nothing from Drew. Apart from a glimpse of his black BMW leaving the manor house on various occasions, she hadn't even seen him. But even more ominous, on another level, was the silence from Greg.

He'd made no further efforts to arrange the Chinese meal, which had come as no surprise after Drew's behaviour. But a meeting to discuss his plans with Drew had been fixed for Friday, and they'd parted quite amicably, and spoken on the phone once or twice. Then, out of the blue on Friday morning, Greg had rung to postpone the meeting, with no explanation. As the days had gone by, she'd rung his number, but no one had answered.

Charlotte was so strung up and impatient, she felt she would go prematurely grey with worry, but the mirror instead showed the familiar pale cheeks and dark-shadowed green eyes she'd grown sick of seeing, and was too dispirited to do anything about. She'd put in hours of work in readiness for building this trimaran—every supplier she could think of had been teed up ready—moulds, carbon fibre, resin. . . She could hardly bring herself to believe Drew had deliberately sabotaged the whole thing. . .surely he wasn't *that* ruthless?

Pride stopped her from ringing Drew, and asking him about Greg. Their last meeting still brought heat to her face whenever she thought about it. She'd been avoiding him ever since. She didn't want to see him, and she dreaded bumping into him. Worse still, if she rang him about Greg, and Drew wasn't involved in his disappearance, he'd know something had gone wrong with her project. The thought of his barely concealed triumph, tinged with pity, was more than she could contemplate. Everything seemed to be in a mess.

'It's the VAT on leisure craft that's killed boat-building,' Geoff intoned, propping himself against a desk in the office during his afternoon tea-break. 'That and the economic recession.'

'I thought there was supposed to be an economic boom?' Charlotte queried drily, scanning the depressing state of the balance sheets to the desultory tapping of Delia's typewriter.

'Oh, aye, for some there is. But leisure craft are still a luxury, Charlie. First to go when there's a bit of a squeeze on.'

How was Greg Smithson's economic situation? she wondered bleakly, driving home that evening after a late session with the accounts. Did Greg have an unexpected 'squeeze' on? Had he decided to abandon his hopes of entering the transatlantic race because he'd run out of funds? Or had Drew told him Wells Boats were on the way out, and he would be advised to take his drawings somewhere else? Her jokey flirtation with Greg on the boat might have triggered a bout of vindictiveness. The month's deadline was nearly up. Maybe it had just been a joke in the first place, so Drew could have the satisfaction of seeing her running round in circles and falling flat on her face? The suspicions circled round in her head until she wanted to scream.

Driving down the long, narrow track towards the manor house, she could see smoke coming from the chimney of Cormorant Cottage. Mrs Bolton had obviously been in, and lit the fire. She felt a small stab of guilt at the sybaritic existence she was allowing herself to lead, with her cottage cleaned, her clothes ironed, even casseroles mysteriously finding their way into the oven. Drew's housekeeper seemed to have developed a stubbornly soft spot for Charlotte, and, short of offending her by forbidding her entry, she couldn't do much about it. If she was perfectly honest with herself, she was guiltily enjoying the pampering. Which was galling, considering who was behind it all. . .

There was a strange car parked outside the manor house as she drove past and triggered the automatic floodlights, a brilliant canary-yellow Morgan, its soft hood recklessly left open under tonight's ominously dark skies. It looked frivolous and exotic next to Drew's sleek, no-nonsense saloon.

She speculated on its possible owner as she let herself into the cottage and kicked her trainers into the hall cupboard. It was none of her business, of course. Any more than a guest's car outside Cormorant Cottage would be Drew's. She flicked the kettle on, and subsided in an exhausted heap in front of the welcoming log fire, giving a heartfelt vote of thanks to Mrs Bolton. The aroma of lavender wax and pine logs was indescribably good to come home to, in spite of all the tensions associated with this place.

Her head ached abominably tonight, and her neck felt stiff and strained from endless hours poring over figures. She leaned back against the sofa, waves of sleepiness engulfing her. The hours spent tossing anxiously through the nights were taking their toll. She'd been dropping asleep as soon as she sat down in the evenings. This time, she woke to the shrill ring of the telephone, and she jumped up, disorientated, still half asleep, hoping it would be Greg, and hearing instead Fiona's high, cool voice on the end of the line.

'Hi, darling. Have I caught you at an awkward moment?'

'No. . .if I sound strange, I was fast asleep a second ago. The phone woke me!'

'Fast asleep—Charlie, it's only half-past nine!'

'Is it?' Charlotte chewed her lip, gazing at the dark water outside the window, and waiting for her sister to say why she'd rung.

'I've got some news, darling. I'm not sure if you're going to like it. . .'

Charlotte took a deep breath, her stomach twisting in knots.

'I had lunch with the *dishy* Drew Meredith this week,' Fiona went on blithely, 'and he's made me an offer I can't refuse!'

Her hand was suddenly damp on the receiver. Not Fiona and Drew, she pleaded silently, please lord, not Fiona and Drew. . .From somewhere in the distance, Charlotte had the nasty feeling Fiona was enjoying keeping her in suspense. Gripping the telephone harder, she braced herself for the worst.

'He's buying my shares in the boatyard.'

Charlotte was speechless, and after a long pause Fiona said tetchily, 'I need the ready cash—I'm buying a bigger flat. And he's offered me a brilliant price!'

'I'll bet he has!' Charlotte managed to say grimly.

'Drew just likes to have power. Now there's no danger of my persuading you to see things my way. Oh, he's a clever operator. And he's a double-crossing. . .' Words briefly failed her. Here was proof of Drew's machinations, behind her back. What an idiot she'd been to contemplate trusting him!

'Mmm—well, I agree I wouldn't want to meet him on a dark night. . .' Fiona laughed lightly '. . .but I do adore men like that, don't you? The brooding, macho type! Frankly, Charlie, I think he's the most attractive man I've ever met. I could get seriously interested in Drew Meredith! We lunched at Ali's Bistro, and every female in the place was cricking her neck to look at him!'

'I'm glad you enjoyed yourself. . .Fiona, can I ask you a straight question? Do you really hate me?'

There was a short pause.

'Of course I don't hate you, Charlie! What a ridiculous question. You're my big sister—I'm very fond of you!' Fiona's brisk reply was totally in character, but Charlotte found herself gripped with an urgent desire to understand her sister's mentality.

'Then why are you doing everything you can to hurt me?' Charlotte demanded simply. 'Whatever happened to family loyalty, Fee?'

'I don't set great store by *family loyalty*,' Fiona retorted levelly. 'I believe in speaking my mind. And I believe in looking after number one! I definitely don't believe in being a martyr to a lost cause! Mum and I were alike on that score!'

'So what was Mother's lost cause? Was it Dad? Or maybe it was me? Is that why she had an affair? Because she believed in looking after "number one"?' Charlotte wished she could retract the bitter words, but it was too late. But Fiona surprised her.

'If you're trying to shock me, I already know about that! I also know who the man was—do you?'

'No. . . Jocelyn didn't think I needed to know. The man's dead. . .'

'True, but it's interesting information all the same. Mother was having a fling with Guy Benedict!'

'Drew's father. . .?' Charlotte felt sick. She sat down abruptly on the chair by the phone, a ghastly fear suddenly gnawing at her stomach. 'Mother and *Guy Benedict*? When did. . . I mean, how long ago did it begin?'

'It's all right—we're not related to Drew, if that's what you're worrying about!' Fiona said with a cynical laugh.

Charlotte felt a wave of heat engulf her, then drain away, leaving her deathly cold. She'd had no tea, she reminded herself impatiently. She ought to know better. People shouldn't receive shocks like this on an empty stomach.

'Fee, how do you know all this?'

'Mum told me about Guy Benedict, herself. But when I found out he was Drew's father, I talked to Drew about it. I asked him straight out—were we our father's daughters, or had his father followed his previous form in such matters, and hit the jackpot again with Mum!'

'Fiona! For pity's sake!' Charlotte was stunned.

'What are you so shocked about? Mum's having an affair, or the fact that she had an affair with Guy Benedict?'

'Both, I suppose. . . I can't take in this latest news at all!'

'Mum was only human, you know. Frankly I think she knew she only had a few years left after that cancer operation. So she decided to grab what life offered! The trouble with you is you expect people to behave like paragons. You put them on pedestals, then you can't understand it when they crash to the ground! It's the same with me, isn't it? I'm supposed to act like your sweet little sister, but instead I know a damn sight more about life than you ever will! Take me or leave me, I really don't care!'

Charlotte's throat was dry. She took a deep breath, and forced herself to stand up again. She'd asked for this, hadn't she? Fee was probably right— she was a naïve, romantic idiot, gullible to the point of stupidity. Maybe it was time she and Fiona fished their hostilities out into the open and examined them objectively.

But right now, she was preoccupied with another bone of contention. Fiona's brand of straight talking had opened her eyes to what was going on around her, and she felt a burning anger consuming her.

Drew had set himself up as some kind of misguided guardian of her safety, since Dad had died. But he was just a natural bully. He had a power-complex worthy of a psychiatrist's couch. He wanted to keep her under his control, manipulate her by making promises he never intended to keep. To her face, he'd been overbearing and arrogant. Behind her back, he'd been meeting Fee and offering her a fortune for her shares, and cleverly removing Greg from the scene, so he could get his own way.

'Will you excuse me now, Fee?' she said chokingly. 'There's someone I need to see.'

She crashed the receiver back in place, pushed her feet rapidly into her trainers, and then she was running through the dark gardens, towards the lights of the manor house.

CHAPTER EIGHT

'IS THERE something the matter, Charlotte dear?'

Mrs Bolton's welcoming smile changed to a frown as she took in Charlotte's flushed cheeks and distraught expression.

'Is he here?' Charlotte's voice shook in the effort to speak civilly to the kindly Mrs Bolton.

'Yes, but he's with someone. . .' The housekeeper's voice trailed away as Charlotte strode towards the drawing-room, pushed open the door, and marched in ready to do battle.

Then she stopped dead in her tracks.

Drew was sitting on the wide sofa by the fireplace, coolly elegant in a grey suit and white silk shirt, his long legs stretched out in front of him, and beside him, leaning intimately towards him, was a beautiful, olive-skinned woman, her arms linked round his neck as she kissed him, laughingly, on the cheek.

'Charlotte. . .' Drew disengaged himself from the woman, and got unhurriedly to his feet, his expression saturnine. 'What a nice surprise,' he murmured. 'Let me introduce you to Melina Patterson——'

'Don't bother introducing us!' Charlotte snapped, goaded beyond civility. 'If she's a friend of yours, she definitely won't be a friend of mine!'

'Charlie. . .' Drew spoke warningly, but she

closed her ears to the implicit threat. Drew wasn't
going to fool her, or control her, or push her around
any longer.

'Fiona just rang me! I gather you've arranged to
buy her shares? So good of you to tell me!' Her
voice broke slightly, but she ploughed on, 'I suppose
you thought you'd get that sorted out before I
realised Greg Smithson had disappeared from the
scene? So now you can do exactly what you want
with my father's company. There's no fear of Fiona
siding with me, and stopping your expansion plans
for the sea school, is there? And since you've so
cleverly engineered Greg Smithson out of the way,
there's no need to humour me any longer! I might
as well give everyone at the boatyard a month's
notice in the morning! Or would you prefer a week?'

Melina Patterson wore a perplexed expression as
she listened to this passionate outburst, her shining
curtain of black hair swinging to and fro as she
looked quickly from Drew to Charlotte. She stood
up, putting an elegant hand on Drew's arm. 'Drew,
darling, would it be better if I left you alone?'

'No!' Drew's deep voice was sharp, his anger
patently obvious as he glared ruthlessly at Charlotte.
'I said I wanted you to meet Charlotte, Melina. Now
you have. And Charlotte is going to apologise for
being so damned rude——'

'Go to hell!' Charlotte exploded, heat rushing to
her face. 'You sanctimonious. . .conceited. . .
insufferable. . .' Suitable expletives failed her, and
she swung round towards the door. 'I don't want to

talk to you again, I don't even want to see you again.
I've had enough!'

She should have felt better after this satisfying
attack, but as she strode back out of the manor
house into the darkness she felt ten times worse.
The shock of seeing Drew with the other woman
had cut like a knife in an old wound. No matter how
much anger she'd off-loaded just now, the image of
the two of them, embracing in front of the fireplace,
refused to fade. Was this the owner of the pink satin
nightdress? The female interior designer, back from
abroad?

She didn't know, and she didn't care. Drew probably had a whole string of willing females, available
for intimate suppers and only too eager to bolster
his monstrous ego by doing exactly what they were
told. Tonight she didn't feel she could ever care
about anything, ever again. She felt as if she'd
reached breaking-point.

Her exodus from Cormorant Cottage was rapid
and haphazard. The prospect of Drew's angry
appearance made her snatch one or two belongings
in frenetic haste, and bundle herself into the car like
a fugitive. But she had to escape. She had to get
away from him—how could she bear to live in his
cottage, a few yards from his manor house, knowing
how he'd duped her? With Fiona, with Greg, and
now with this woman called Melina. . .

The rain came sweeping in from the west as she
drove back towards Shalmouth, and she slowed
down, the windscreen wipers battling against the

sudden deluge, tears pouring down her cheeks and blinding her almost as much as the rain. With any luck the glamorous Melina Patterson would have forgotten the hood of her Morgan was down, and the canary-yellow sports car would be awash when she went out to it. The petty spitefulness of that thought brought an involuntary smile through her tears. She was behaving badly tonight, and the knowledge was oddly comforting. Fiona's reference to martyrs had caught her on the raw. Was that how she saw her? Was that how she'd been behaving until now?

She drove without a conscious destination in mind, but she found herself heading for the seafront, making for the boatyard. She had her sleeping-bag in the boot, and the office keys in the glove compartment of her car. The floor wouldn't be the most comfortable bed for the night, but she didn't feel up to Fiona's supercilious company, and it was too late in the evening to inflict her emotional problems on Susie.

She was nearly there when the spluttering of the engine dashed her spirits even further. The car hiccuped to a standstill half a mile from the docks, and no amount of persuasion would coax it back to life again. Fool, she cursed herself furiously, quelling the overwhelming urge to get out and kick the ancient vehicle. If she was determined to demonstrate her fierce independence tonight, she could at least have had a reliable car to do so in style.

There was nothing else for it, she would have to

walk the rest of the way. If she went back into town to find a garage, she would get soaked in any case, and she could ring someone from the boatyard. With the rain still lashing down, she scrambled around to the boot, retrieving her waxed jacket and thanking the gods that her sleeping-bag was in the waterproof case she used when she took it sailing. Locking the car, she abandoned it at the side of the road and set off at a jog along the sea front, with the rain rapidly soaking her hair and pouring in chilly rivulets down her neck.

The docks were dark and deserted, except for a group of sailors lurching out of the public bar of the Beach Inn, making their way back to their cargo ship. One of them called something to her, either in a foreign language or a strong regional accent, she couldn't tell, and she was in no mood to stop and find out. She kept her head down as she strode past them, hearing their raucous shouts with a plunging heart.

She became aware of the footsteps behind her as she neared the other side of the docks and turned the corner into the shadowy courtyard of Wells Boats. Sudden, irrational fear engulfed her, and with the hairs prickling on the back of her neck she began to run, her trainers making no sound on the cobbles, the following footsteps ringing steadily somewhere behind.

By the time she flew up the rickety wooden steps to the office, and fumbled for the key, the adrenalin was pumping through her body so violently she felt geared up to fighting off half a dozen assailants. But she would be no match for a man's superior strength, her instincts warned her, as she flung open the door and dived inside. As she did so, the key slipped from her fingers and fell down through the slatted wooden platform, tinkling mockingly as it reached the cobbles below. In horror, she almost fell inside the office and slammed the door, dragging a chair over to wedge beneath the handle and then huddling down in the shadows, breathing heavily, her heart pounding like a piston after her headlong flight.

Brilliant, she told herself scathingly, as she strained her ears to hear if the footsteps had continued to follow her. She was holed up in a pitch-dark boatyard, and she couldn't even lock herself in for safety. She dared not put on the light, in case the prowler saw her and grew bolder. The telephone was on the other side of the room, and she would have to pass the window to get to it. Belatedly, she recalled incidents of assaults and muggings in the dockyard area. Susie had been relating another newspaper report, only a few days ago. What kind of an idiot was she, to walk right into a situation like this?

She had no idea how long she crouched there, cold and wet, alone in the darkness. But when soft footsteps sounded on the wooden steps outside, she felt at first paralysed with fright, then furiously angry. No man was going to assault her—he would be sorry he tried. Her fingers closed instinctively round the first weapon which came to hand—a heavy brass ashtray from the shelf behind her. Heart in mouth, she watched a shadowy figure loom threateningly through the glass, trying the handle, discovering the unlocked door with the chair propped behind it. Almost sobbing with fear, she stifled her desire to scream as the figure withdrew for a moment then kicked the door with such violent force it flew wide open, letting in a shower of rain and a blast of cold night air.

Charlotte leapt to her feet with a shout, and swung the ashtray with all her might, and the low grunt of pain told her she'd hit her target.

But the moment of victory was shortlived. She was abruptly clamped in an efficient half-nelson, the ashtray falling to the floor with a dull thud, and she sobbed and kicked and fought like a wildcat while the intruder spun round and flicked the light switch, hauling her round to face him.

'Drew!'

'Charlotte, you've nearly concussed me! What in the devil's name do you think you're doing?'

'What were *you* doing, kicking the door in like that? I almost died of fright!'

'How the hell was I to know you'd be hiding behind the door with all the lights off?'

She stared at him, dazedly, suddenly aware that she was trembling violently all over, in the aftermath of fear. 'Oh, Drew!' Crumpling at the knees, she fell against him. And then, to her eternal chagrin, she burst into tears. Once started, she found it hard to stop. There was a degree of hysteria creeping in as he closed his arms round her and gave her a gentle shake.

'Are you all right, Charlotte?' His voice was urgent. 'No one's attacked you. . .?'

'No. Only you,' she amended shakily, dragging her wits together with an immense effort and fumbling in her pocket for a tissue.

'I thought it was the other way round?'

'Self-defence. . .' She sniffed, scrubbing at her tear-blotched face. 'I passed a crowd of drunks. . .then I heard footsteps behind me, and. . .and I panicked. I ran up here, but I dropped the key before I could lock the door behind me. . .'

'When I saw your car abandoned half a mile back, all sorts of gruesome scenes started appearing in my mind! I've been off my head with worry!' His voice was rough as he crushed her to him, and tilted her chin up to meet his angry gaze. 'Were you planning to spend the *night* here?'

'Yes. . .' There was a drop of blood trickling down his temple, she realised, aghast. 'Drew, your face is bleeding. . .'

'I'm not surprised. You could have killed me with that damned ashtray!'

There was a moment's silence, and they faced each other warily. In spite of her chilled body, a heat was beginning to kindle between them, and she wriggled in his arms, anxious to escape before she disgraced herself any further.

'Let me go, Drew. I'm all right now. I'll get some water to bathe your head. . .'

'I'm not letting you go,' his voice deepened, his body heat starting to thaw her stiff limbs, 'and you're coming back to the manor house with me, right now——'

'No! Drew, I'm not——'

Before she could say any more, he jerked her roughly against him, bent his head and kissed her, hard, on the mouth. She hadn't time to fight. Nor did she have the inclination. The response was instantaneous. The temperature rose so abruptly between them, she was utterly lost. The raw, impatient passion of his kiss was irresistible, firing her stomach with a fierce, almost painful ache of desire. As she gave a choked cry, her hands crept up to his shoulders, clinging possessively to the damp cloth of his trenchcoat, and as his kiss grew more demanding her mouth opened hungrily beneath the pressure.

'Oh, Drew. . .' She surfaced for breath, whispering his name against his lips, her breath mingling with his, filled with such a nameless yearning that she was quivering inside. If she shut her mind to reality, she could pretend none of the past quarrels had happened. The conflict over the boatyard, the string of other women, the distrust Drew had always shown in her behaviour with other men. . . She could even imagine Drew had always loved her, the way she'd always loved him. . .

'Do as you're told, and come home with me!' There was a brilliant glitter of triumph beneath the sensual droop of his eyelids, and she stared up at him, captured in that glittering gaze. Breathing seemed to be suspended as their eyes locked in silence. The harsh overhead office light cast strong shadows over his face. The door was still open, swinging in the wind, and small flurries of rain were blowing in.

But they stood, motionless, oblivious to everything around them.

'Drew. . . I just——'

He put a finger against her lips, shaking his head abruptly. 'Just be quiet. I intend to talk and you're going to listen. But first I get you somewhere warm and out of those wet clothes. . .'

He was so decisive, and she felt so pole-axed by the intensity of emotion she'd just experienced, that for once she let him take charge without a murmur of dissent. Her earlier ordeal had shaken her up more than she realised, but it was debatable if that was the reason her legs felt weak as he guided her firmly down to the car.

She subsided into the passenger seat, silently marvelling that in Drew's company the shadowy courtyard no longer held any threat.

'That's an improvement—you've stopped arguing,' he murmured wryly, flicking a sidelong glance at her as they swept through the rain-washed streets of the town. 'Or are you just recharging your batteries for the next assault?'

He was pushing her around again, she recognised grimly. Giving orders. The self-sufficient skipper in charge of the boat, brooking no insubordination.

But she leaned back and closed her eyes, suddenly too exhausted to continue with the fight. She hated to admit it, but just for once the notion of someone else taking charge of her life seemed quite attractive.

Half an hour later, she was showered and changed and warming up in front of the fire in Cormorant Cottage, huddled in her towelling robe, sipping the mug of hot cocoa Drew had produced when she had come downstairs. The atmosphere between Drew and herself had become oddly constrained, and she wondered if he was feeling as confused as she was. He'd said he had some talking to do, that she was going to listen. She dreaded hearing what he had to say. The truth was sometimes so painful, it was better not said.

She took a sip of cocoa, and cast a veiled glance towards Drew where he sat, broodingly, on the chair opposite, his shirt collar and tie loosened, his dark curls still damp from the rain. He'd foregone the cocoa, and had poured himself a stiff whisky. He was so achingly attractive she wanted to cry.

At last, they both began to speak at once, and both stopped. She felt colour seep into her cheeks, and she looked quickly down into the fire again.

'This is bloody ridiculous!' Drew said abruptly, standing up and beginning to prowl around the room. 'It's much easier talking to you when we're arguing! Seeing you sitting there so prim and demure has totally thrown me!'

'You told me to be quiet,' she reminded him levelly, doing her best to keep the tell-tale shake out of her voice. 'You said you had some talking to do, and I was going to listen. Frankly I think this is a complete waste of time, but go ahead, I'm waiting.'

'Tonight I finally realised something. . .' Drew was looking hunted. 'Things can't go on like this. . .'

'I quite agree!' She was slowly dying inside. Why had she fallen in love with him all over again? Why couldn't she just hate him, the way she ought to?

'I can't go on pretending, Charlie——'

'You don't have to!' she burst out, chokingly. 'All you have to do is stop feeling so *guilty* about me! Because that's all it is, isn't it?'

'Guilty about you? What are you talking about?'

'Oh, stop trying to pretend! I suppose Melina Patterson is the female interior decorator who decorated Cormorant Cottage, isn't she?'

'Yes, she is, but——'

'So in the absence of Delia, or. . .or Fiona, or heaven knows what other women you have in tow, you had plenty to occupy your time tonight! Why did you bother to come looking for me, Drew?'

'Because I intended talking some sense into your head! And because I care about what happens to you!'

'Oh, forget the act! Admit it, you don't care a damn what happens to me. . .and why the hell should you? I see it all clearly now—you've had this misguided impression that, because of your friendship with Dad, I'm someone you ought to feel responsible for. . .a kind of emotional embarrassment. . .but I'm not! I've long outgrown that stupid crush I had on you! And I was wrong to ask you for favours over the boatyard—Fee's right, business is business, no room for *sentiment*! I had no right to expect you to care. . .so you can drop the pretence, stop humouring me to my face and conducting business as usual behind my back——!'

The torrent of words choked off in a furious sob, as Drew strode over to her, taking her by the shoulders, shaking her roughly.

'Will you stop? You're talking rubbish! I've always cared what happens to you! If I hadn't cared about you, it would have been only too easy to take what was on offer five years ago, Charlie! Hell, did you think I didn't *want* to?'

'Yes, that's the impression you gave! If you wanted me, why didn't you *take* me?' She was almost sobbing with anger.

'I've told you why! You were *seventeen* years old, Charlie! I was a friend of your father's! But if I didn't care about you, why do you think I felt so murderous when I saw you with Colin? Why do you think I wanted to garrotte your smooth-talking Greg Smithson a couple of weeks ago?'

She stared at him speechlessly. Drew's fingers were digging mercilessly into her shoulders, and she bit her lip. Her legs were shaking. She yearned for him so desperately, she thought she might melt into a jelly.

'I want you. . .you must know that!' His eyes searched her face hungrily. 'I can't sleep at night any more, thinking about you. . .'

The panic jolted through her like an enormous electric shock.

'Drew, I can't. . . I'm sorry!' It was almost a whisper, and he frowned at her blackly, bending his head to catch her words. She felt tears prick her eyelids, and held her breath while she fought for control.

'What are you saying, Charlie?' His voice was agonised.

'I'm saying. . . I'm saying. . .' she swallowed convulsively '. . .I'm no good at. . .at casual sex! I know it's there—this. . .this physical need between us, but it's no good for me——'

'Casual sex? For crying out loud!' He dropped his hands from her shoulders, raking unsteady fingers through his hair. 'If I wanted casual sex I'd have helped myself years ago! I'm trying to tell you I love you! I need you! I can't live without you! I'm asking you to marry me, Charlotte!'

CHAPTER NINE

'MARRY you?' If Charlie had felt a wave of panic before, now she was swamped in it. She went hot and cold in turn. 'Marry you? Is this a joke, Drew?'

'It's no joke!' He was watching her reaction with such ferocious intensity, she felt mesmerised.

'We couldn't possibly marry! It's the weirdest suggestion I've ever heard!' she blurted out at last, not looking at him.

'Why?'

'For a start, marriage needs trust!'

'We can work on that——'

'You've deliberately tried to sabotage my plan to revive Wells Boats, just so you can knock it down and build your precious marina. . . You expect me to *trust* you?'

Drew had dropped his hands from her shoulders, gazing at her with the now familiar deadpan expression as she paused for breath.

'Go on. Finish the list of accusations.'

'All right. . .you've. . .you've got double standards. You've got a. . .a harem of women, but if I go in for a spot of light flirtation I'm called every name under the sun——'

'What *harem* of women?' His wide mouth was twisted in wry humour, she noticed distractedly.

How could he find something to laugh about, during such a vital conversation?

'Delia, Fiona, Melina Patterson. . .'

She trailed off, her cheeks flushed with passion, her heart thumping angrily, and he waited for a moment, eyebrows raised expectantly.

'Is that it?' he queried, when she said nothing more. 'Do I get a chance to defend myself now? Let's start with the boatyard. I'm not the black villain you seem to think. Greg Smithson has been toying with a competitive tender from Fennel Boats. . .'

'I don't believe you! Tim Fennel's an old school-friend of mine, and he'd never——'

'Don't be naïve! Old schoolfriends are just like any other competitor in business, Charlie! I've spent the past fortnight tripping over myself to *save* your contract with Smithson.' Drew's eyes glittered cold suddenly, his smile nowhere near reaching them. 'Which, considering you declared I was "bloody distasteful" to you last time we were together, was fairly noble of me, don't you think?'

She pushed her wildly tumbled curls back from her face, eyeing him warily. 'Why didn't you tell me this was going on? I've been out of my mind worrying!'

'I got the impression you were avoiding me like the proverbial plague since our little fiasco in Hamble.' His glance was sardonic. Charlotte looked down at the glowing logs in the fire, her emotions in a confused muddle.

'As for this harem I'm accused of running, I'm not claiming I've lived the life of a monk, Charlotte. But I've never laid a finger on Delia. The passion there is entirely one-sided, unchivalrous though it sounds——'

'Poor Delia. She has my sympathy!' She couldn't avoid the bitter outburst, then regretted it instantly.

'Poor Delia? That girl has made my life hell over the last couple of years! Letters, phone calls, suicide threats——'

'*Suicide* threats? Drew, are you serious?'

'Never more so. Believe me, these infatuations can be lethal!' Drew spoke with quiet conviction, and suddenly Charlotte felt like crying.

'Yes. . .' Coldness was creeping into her. She was remembering how slavishly she'd adored him, how she'd thrown herself at him during that trip to Menorca. She felt rigid with embarrassment. 'Yes. . . I do know all about *infatuation*,' she said quietly, bitterly. 'Maybe I should talk to Delia. At least I can reassure her from my own experience that time is a great healer!'

A wave of dark colour rose in Drew's face, but after a brief pause he went on as if she hadn't spoken.

'Fiona is your sister, and a shareholder in Wells Boats, nothing more. I'm buying her shares because she came to me and asked me to. And Melina Patterson is not only twelve years older than me, she's my half-sister. . .'

Charlotte was stunned. Turning round slowly, she stared at him incredulously. 'Your half-sister?'

'It's a long story.' Drew took a look at her face, and grimaced wryly. 'I met her a few years ago when I was making enquiries about my mother among the Greek-Cypriot community. . . She's been a good friend to me, Charlie.'

'She. . .she lived in Cormorant Cottage?'

'Yes. She was having some trouble with a boyfriend. She wanted to get away from everything for a while.'

'She's not married?'

'No. Melina's a real career woman. She's got her own business. She travels quite a lot. . .' He frowned slightly, loosening his tie a little more and reaching for his whisky glass. 'But meeting her has been very good for me. She could remember things from the past. She's told me things about my real mother. . .'

Drew rubbed his forehead in a sudden gesture of weariness, then thrust his hands into his trouser pockets. 'My mother was already married, with four children, when she met Guy Benedict,' he said, seeing her blank expression. 'Her husband was a sailor in the merchant navy. When he was home he drank a lot and beat her up. Maybe Guy made her happy for a while? I told you once before it's a sordid story. I'm only telling you this to make you see Melina's part in all of it. She was twelve when I was born. She remembers all the anguish.' Drew laughed without humour. 'I suppose I shouldn't draw comfort from knowing my mother was bitterly unhappy, should I? But it seemed important to discover that at least *one* of my real parents wanted me! It made me feel less "rejected"! It sounds bloody ridiculous, I know!'

Charlotte sank down on to her chair again, holding the turquoise folds of the towelling robe closely around her.

'It doesn't sound at all ridiculous. I understand. . .' she said in a low voice.

'Do you?'

'Yes. . .that is, I know how rejection feels. . .as a matter of fact, it's coloured most of my life!' She lifted her head, meeting his eyes with a steady gaze. 'My ego took rather a battering at your hands, five years ago!'

'Charlie. . .' It was an agonised groan, and Drew came over to her in two strides, pulling her to her feet, his hands at her waist. 'Darling Charlie! If you mean what happened between us in Menorca, I didn't *want* to reject you. Oh, hell, this is so complicated, I don't know how to begin!'

'Begin with the truth?' she suggested shakily, wishing she weren't wearing nothing beneath the robe, already aware of the treacherous stirring of her senses at the closeness of Drew's body.

'The truth?' The amber eyes were suddenly clouded, his expression ironic. 'All right. You claim you were "infatuated" with me, years ago? Well, you certainly hid it well! You were the coolest, most self-possessed little tomboy I'd ever come across.

You used to come down to the docks straight from school, remember? A tousled schoolgirl, in a grey gymslip and navy blazer, with the greenest eyes I'd ever seen. You used to give me that straight, unsmiling gaze of yours, and I'd start feeling things I had no right to feel! I thought I was going crazy! After Debbie, I thought I'd learned my lesson. Immature young girls were trouble with a capital "T". But I couldn't get you out of my head. Remember the free sailing lessons I used to give you? Just so I could legitimately be near you for a while!'

'You're making this up. . .' It was a failed attempt at sarcasm, her voice shook too much, and she bit her lip as he ignored her.

'I fought against it, Charlotte. First, you were only fifteen. Way out of bounds! Second, even when you reached the age of legal consent, damn it, the situation reminded me so much of my episode with Debbie, I was bloody terrified! And last but not least. . .there was another possible complication. . .'

Drew hesitated, and she suddenly knew what he was going to say.

'I know about my mother and your father, if that's what you're wondering! Fiona told me tonight. . .'

He pulled a grim face. 'In that case, you know what I'm talking about.'

She felt a wave of heat sweep over her again, then shivered, as she remembered the past. 'You thought we might be brother and sister!'

'Guy told me about his affair with your mother. I

didn't find out for certain until your parents divorced, three years ago. Your father told me he'd demanded blood tests to prove paternity. . .'

There was total silence, and they stared at each other blindly. Then Drew moved to crush her into his arms, taking her by surprise, almost tipping her off balance.

Cupping her chin in one hand, he raised her mouth to his and began to kiss her, very slowly and thoroughly, savouring her with infinite pleasure and exploration until she gasped against his mouth, her stomach on fire, pressing herself helplessly against him.

'Drew. . . I can't think straight. . . I'm not sure what I feel any more. . .'

'I'm very sure how I feel!' he said thickly against her cheek. 'I love you, and I want to marry you, Charlotte. I don't give a damn about the past— when I was searching for you tonight, I realised that I'd die if anything happened to you. . .'

'I don't understand. . .' She writhed closer as he slid his hands down to her hips, pressing her hungrily against him. 'You said you didn't believe in love. You were so. . .hostile in Menorca, that night on the *Menorquina* after the storm. . .and when you saw me with Colin. . .'

He crushed her convulsively to him, his lips in her hair. 'It nearly killed me, getting into that sleeping-bag with you. But if I hadn't you wouldn't be here today, my love! You were so chilled after that spell in the sea, it was literally life or death. There wasn't time for prudishness! I just didn't bank on your demonstrating your. . .deliciously amorous nature quite so. . .irresistibly!' He was kissing her, between the words, and she clung to him, melting, suddenly heady with happiness.

'Drew, do you really mean it? You love me?' She lifted her head and smiled luminously up at him.

'I can't think of any other explanation for why I've been back-tracking on a profitable business plan to humour you, why I've been obsessed with making sure you have a safe roof over your head, and why I have this urge to disembowel any male who comes within a two-metre radius of you!' He kissed her hard on the mouth, then fixed her with a look of such blinding heat that she caught her breath. 'Worse still, I can't keep my hands off you! Damn it, Charlie, you've got me so I can't sleep at night. If you don't tell me you love me, I'll probably end up in a strait-jacket!'

She was captured in the glittering gaze. She could hardly breathe. 'I do love you, Drew! You know I do! I think you've always known I do!'

The dark wash of colour stained his face again as he gazed down at her gravely, then he slid his hands up to cup her face, his eyes darkening. 'If you love me, how come you're refusing to marry me?'

'I'm not!' she said, on a shaky laugh, feeling him tense then relax abruptly against her, tightening his hold around her head and threading his fingers into her dark curls.

'Special licence it is, then,' he said quietly, surprising her by disengaging himself abruptly, and holding her at arm's length. The towelling robe had become dishevelled, and his eyes roved down over the parts of her body revealed to him, lingering hungrily until she felt hot and breathless and melting with desire.

'And what do you say to a honeymoon in Menorca?' His voice had deepened and roughened.

'Menorca?' She stared at him, nonplussed, then she read the cool determination in his eyes, and gradually his meaning began to sink in. 'Menorca. . .yes, that would be lovely, Drew. . .' She couldn't move. Her legs were so boneless she was almost collapsing. Her heart was bumping crazily in her chest. She could hardly breathe.

'Good. . .' He scooped her to him, kissing her finally with a measured passion which made her senses swim, then pulling the edges of the robe together and belting it firmly round her waist, his eyes unfathomable. 'We have some unfinished business in Menorca, Charlie.'

It was strange, thought Charlotte, sifting hot sand through her fingers and dozing in the shade of a beach umbrella, how a particular smell could trigger half a dozen memories. The scent of these pine trees, giving off their heady fragrance in the midday sun, seemed to have turned the clock back five years. Those heart-stopping days, when she'd yearned so hopelessly for Drew, yet hidden it valiantly in the company of Colin, and Antonia, and

Griff. . .it all seemed as real as if she were back there, seventeen, in the throes of the most painful calf-love imaginable. . . Was that why Drew had insisted they come here? To exorcise ghosts?

She sat up on her comfortable beach bed, dusted the fine white sand off her fingers and reached for the sun oil, inspecting the slender curve of her thighs for signs of burning. Normally she tanned fast, but they'd just arrived an hour ago, and this was the hottest time of day. She smoothed more oil on the danger-zone where her mint-green swim-suit was cut high on the groin, added an extra coating to her upper arms, throat and breasts where the deep scoop neck revealed vulnerable white skin, then relaxed back on her forearms, eyeing her surroundings with deep satisfaction.

The villa Drew had brought her to belonged to a friend of his who owned various holiday villages on the island. It was difficult to find, and even more of a problem to get to, requiring half an hour's bumpy drive off the main road from Mahon to Ciudadela, in a hired Jeep, along pot-holed tracks which blazed clouds of dust in their wake. But, once there, it was worth the discomfort. Built around a huge sapphire-blue pool, it stood alone, surrounded by arid farm-land criss-crossed with hundreds of dry-stone walls, and it had arched white walls clad in shocking pink bougainvillaea and white hibiscus, and plenty of shady date palms and banana palms shimmering in the steady breeze off the sea. Even more satisfac-tory, it possessed its own private cove. And the jewel in its crown, as far as Charlotte was concerned, was the fifty-foot luxury yacht moored a hundred metres from the shore, glistening like white icing against the blue water, its mainsail furled, bobbing gently at anchor. They could forget the Jeep and the donkey-track, Drew had grinned, as they had unloaded their cases. The rest of the island was simply a short sail away

'What do you think of the place?'

Drew had emerged through the sand-dunes, clad only in extremely well-worn white denim Bermudas, and a pair of Raybans. In one hand was balanced a circular silver tray, bearing a bottle and two glasses.

'I used to think Antonia's villa was the last word in luxury until I came here!' She watched him approach, her eyes lingering on the powerful hardness of his body, as he placed the tray on the small table between them.

'Next time we come it could be ours. The villa and the sloop out there. Would you like that?'

'*Drew*! Are you teasing me?'

His wide mouth twisted as he sat on the adjacent beach bed. 'I'm not teasing you. My old friend Ramon Fernandez would sell me anything I want—at the right price, of course! He's been on to me for years to set up a sailing school in one of his holiday complexes. . .just a thought for the future, if we ever get too depressed with the Shalmouth rain. *Te gustaría champán, Señora Meredith*?'

The glow hadn't yet diminished from being called by her newly married name. Her fingers went instinctively to the large solitaire diamond with its matching gold band on her finger, and she sat up, flushed with dazed pleasure, laughing up at him. '*Sí, Señor Meredith, me gustaría muchísimo!*'

'*Bueno, aquí está.*' Drew poured champagne into two glasses with a flourish and handed one to her, tipping their rims together and smiling darkly. She wished she could see his eyes. 'And since our Spanish is so amazingly good, I think we should go somewhere tonight and talk to the natives!'

'If you like. . .' She was non-committal. She was aware of a constraint between them, and she knew the reason for it, on her part at least. The prospect of the coming night was looming ahead, tantalising yet terrifying. Suddenly, now she was actually Drew's wife, the thought of making love with him was giving her butterflies in her stomach. She wondered if he'd sensed her diffidence? He was putting no pressure on her. He hadn't leapt on her the second they had closed the villa door. . .had she half expected him to? Half hoped he would? Did he still find her attractive? His restraint since the moment she'd said she would marry him had been exemplary, and there'd been so much to do, so many arrangements to make in the lightning two weeks before their wedding, she'd refrained from questioning him too closely. Besides, she'd been too shy. Past rejections died hard, she reflected uneasily. To demand why Drew didn't want to make love to her right then and there was simply impossible.

She took a sip of the chilled champagne, and

closed her eyes, mocking herself. She'd started off being miffed by his immaculate self-control, now she was fretting over the imminent event! What on earth was wrong with her?

'I've you to thank for my meagre ability in Spanish!' she laughed, toying with her glass and avoiding his eyes as he watched her. 'I was so impressed by your fluency last time we were here, I went to conversation classes while I was at university.'

'From now on the tuition is free.' The deep voice held an inflexion which made the colour seep into her face. She stared out over the infinite blue of the bay, panic washing through her again. She felt gripped with such nervous apprehension, she could hardly believe it.

'Charlie. . .darling. . .' He came to squat on his haunches by her beach bed, flipping the Raybans off. His eyes were grave and yet somehow full of laughter as well. 'Relax, my love. We've had too much build-up to this, haven't we? Now we're like a couple of kids on their first date.'

The relief was so immense. She sat up and reached out her arms to him, and he slid his own gently round her, holding her tenderly. 'I love you,' he said softly against her hair. 'We've got all the time in the world to get to know each other better. Stop looking at me as if I'm going to turn into a ravening sex maniac, and come and have a swim?'

'I'll race you out to the sloop!'

Slamming her glass down, she had a head start. Drew had to stop to take off his Bermudas. She was nearly there when he overtook her, his powerful crawl slicing through the water almost soundlessly. Up the ladder and on to the deck, and they rested, glistening and panting, laughing at each other.

'You're a strong swimmer.'

'Nearly as strong as you!' She grinned at him, shielding her eyes against the glare of the water. 'That's probably what saved my life that night of the storm!'

'Possibly. That, and my timely intervention with the hypothermia treatment,' Drew reminded her softly, his eyes suddenly sobering on the sleek swell of her shoulders above the wet swim-suit, the taut jut of her nipples through the clinging fabric.

Idiotically shy, she turned on to her stomach, propping herself on her elbows.

'You've begun to tan already,' he murmured huskily, reaching out to slide the strap down and reveal the paler skin beneath, 'It's good seeing you fit and relaxed. You've looked like one of Mrs Bolton's ghosts these last few weeks. . .'

'Not that bad, surely?'

'Fairly bad. You've had a rough time, darling. Partly at my hands. . .' Drew pushed the wet curls from her cheek with a gentle finger, his narrowed gaze searching her face intently. 'I'm sorry I was such a swine over the boatyard, Charlie. . .'

'You weren't. . .' She bit her lip, hesitating. 'I was just as hostile as you were. . .it seemed the last straw, somehow. Dad dying, then having to face you again as a *business* partner, and trying to pretend I didn't care about you any more. . .' Her voice dried up, and he leaned over, pushing her wet hair out of the way, and kissed the nape of her neck.

'I know now how much your father's boatyard means to you, Charlie. I want you to have it—I'll finance it, you can run it.'

'Oh, Drew, there's no need——'

'Look on it as a wedding present.'

'I don't need presents. The best present in my life is finding we're not enemies any longer. . .'

Drew's long brown fingers were tracing a pattern across the narrow curve of her back, and now they travelled lower, lightly circling the deep plunge of the swim-suit where it covered her buttocks.

'We've never exactly been enemies,' he said huskily, 'but I was shattered, seeing you again when you came back to Shalmouth. . . I'd almost forgotten the effect you had on me. . .and then you were so cold and disdainful, I confess I got knotted up with pride!'

'So did I. I thought you hated me!'

'Just shows how wrong you can be.'

Her stomach was starting to do strange things, as Drew's skilful fingers continued their light exploration. Charlotte felt her breathing become more rapid, and turning her head she met his eyes with a steady, challenging gaze which ignited an answering light in Drew's.

'Do you mind very much if I become a ravening sex maniac, Charlie?' The heat in his eyes, and the roughness in his voice were almost more arousing than his touch.

'No. . .' She was breathless, filled with sudden sure knowledge of what she wanted, and she slid the other strap of her swim-suit down, and then kneeled up, peeling the costume down to her waist and crouching, unashamed, in front of him. 'In fact, I'd quite like you to, Drew. . .'

Drew stood up, his own breathing far from steady. Through veiled eyes she watched his dark height and daunting physique as he bent to draw her up with him, cupping her damp breasts in his hands and stroking the hotly budding nipples with his thumbs, his eyes grave as he bent to flick his tongue over each rosy nub. She was so weak and melting for him, his mouth was like a drug she'd been denied for too long. With his fingers in her wet hair, he lifted his head at last from her breasts, and held her face still while he took possession of her lips, his tongue delving gradually further and harder inside her mouth until she caved in, slipping trembling hands round his back and pressing herself helplessly against him.

'Drew, I want you so much. . .' She was half sobbing against his lips, out of her mind with desire, feeling the shudder ricochet through him as their bodies came into full contact, her breasts pressed against his chest, the hardness of his arousal probing the softness of her stomach. Suddenly everything seemed to spin out of control. There seemed to be no time to think, there was just this pulsing need to feel Drew's large, warm hands taking possession of every inch of her body, to peel away the last scraps of clothing and revel in this wondrous nakedness, gasping, whispering, breath mingling, while inside her a curious quivering, swelling feeling seemed to have overwhelmed all other bodily functions.

With a low groan, Drew gathered her in his arms, and elbowed his way down into the double aft-cabin, laying her on the bunk and pressing his face into her stomach, his hands cupping her buttocks, his lips and tongue and fingers exploring every secret crevice of her body until she writhed beneath him, sobbing her need.

'I wanted to do this slowly. . .the right time, the right place, everything perfect!' he growled thickly in her ear, covering her pliant softness with a power-ful lunge, and making a place for himself between her trembling legs. 'But you've made that impossible, my darling!'

'This *is* perfect. . .' she whispered achingly, reaching up to grasp his shoulders, pulling him impatiently down to feel the delicious rasp of his chest hair against her nipples. 'Please, Drew. . .oh, please. . .please! I love you so much, I can't wait any longer. . .'

There was no more talking. With a fierce hunger Drew probed the warm moistness of her, then with brilliant glitter of triumph he thrust inside her, and Charlotte opened her mouth to cry out as the sharp, hot lance of pain jolted her down from the height of her passion, temporarily reducing her to a panic-stricken jelly. Drew had frozen, all movement suspended, and slowly raising his head he looked silently down at her, his golden gaze stunned.

'Charlie. . .' He was shaking his head in slow disbelief. 'Charlie. . .for the love of——' He stopped, rubbing his forehead where a sheen of sweat had broken out beneath the slick of salt water. 'You crazy little. . .Why didn't you *tell* me?'

'Would it have made any difference?'

'Yes, you idiot, I'd have been on my very best behaviour!'

'Then I'm glad I didn't!' She was half laughing, half gasping with the urgent, unbearable excitement streaking through her whole body at this tantalising interruption. 'Oh, Drew, don't stop! Love me, please, please, love me!'

'Charlie. . .' It was a soft, exultant groan against her breast, and then Drew began to move again, gently and with infinite tenderness, and then, as she locked herself wantonly around him, with increasing momentum, his breath warm against her ear as he murmured husky words of love and desire, his lips and hands and the thrust of his body driving her half out of her mind with sensation, and longing, the waves of reaction mounting until suddenly, abruptly her insides seemed to gather together and clench and harden and she cried out in wild, bewildered joy, and the ripples of pleasure spread endlessly from her toes to the top of her head.

There was a slick of perspiration on their bodies

as they lay limply wrapped in each other's arms. Charlotte felt heavy and languorous, her body blissfully feminine and complete. When she finally found the energy to move her hand she trailed her fingers along the hard brown flank beside her, marvelling in the glorious contrast in their bodies, and twisted her head round to look rapturously into Drew's lazy, lidded gaze.

'Well? Did I do all right?'

'Did you do all right?' There was love and laughter, and just a hint of reproach in the deep voice. 'Charlotte, my love, when I exercised noble self-restraint five years ago, and then found you in bed with Colin a few days later, I felt like jumping off the nearest cliff. Can you ever begin to imagine how I feel right now, discovering that I'm the *first*? The first man to make love to my adorable, innocent, shameless, wanton, infinitely lovable wife?'

She laughed softly, twining her arms round him more tightly, and feeling him hardening against her with a fresh stab of longing.

'I told you at the time nothing happened between Colin and me,' she said softly, reasonably. 'Colin would have *liked* something to happen—that's why he climbed into my bed in the early hours, ever hopeful, I suppose. . . I was telling you the truth about that night, but you wouldn't listen. And since then I've never come across a man who made me want to tear all my clothes off and climb into a yacht bunk with him. . . So tell me, how *do* you feel?'

'Like I've just got special dispensation from the

powers above. . .like I've been told I'm going to live forever!'

She frowned, wrapping a thigh around his and feeling the extremely satisfactory result with a delicious shiver of awareness. 'I think we should stick to realistic possibilities. . .what if I said I'll love you forever?'

'I suppose I'd settle for that.'

'Me too.' And she prepared to demonstrate precisely how she intended to keep her side of the bargain.

THIS JULY, HARLEQUIN OFFERS YOU THE PERFECT SUMMER READ!

Sunsational

**EMMA DARCY
EMMA GOLDRICK
PENNY JORDAN
CAROLE MORTIMER**

From top authors of Harlequin Presents comes
HARLEQUIN SUNSATIONAL, a four-stories-in-one
book with 768 pages of romantic reading.

Written by such prolific Harlequin authors as Emma Darcy,
Emma Goldrick, Penny Jordan and Carole Mortimer,
HARLEQUIN SUNSATIONAL is the perfect summer
companion to take along to the beach, cottage, on your
dream destination or just for reading at home in the warm
sunshine!

Don't miss this unique reading opportunity.

Available wherever Harlequin books are sold.

Coming soon
to an easy chair near you.

FIRST CLASS is Harlequin's armchair travel plan for the incurably romantic. You'll visit a different dreamy destination every month from January through December without ever packing a bag. No jet lag, no expensive air fares and *no* lost luggage. Just First Class Harlequin Romance reading, featuring exotic settings from Tasmania to Thailand, from Egypt to Australia, and more.

FIRST CLASS romantic excursions guaranteed! Start your world tour in January. Look for the special **FIRST CLASS** destination on selected Harlequin Romance titles—there's a new one every month.

NEXT DESTINATION:
FLORENCE, ITALY

 Harlequin Books

JTR7

This August, don't miss an exclusive
two-in-one collection of earlier love stories

MAN
WITH A PAST

TRUE COLORS

**by one of today's hottest
romance authors,**

Jayne Ann Krentz

Now, two of Jayne Ann Krentz's most loved books are available together in this special edition that new and longtime fans will want to add to their bookshelves.

Let Jayne Ann Krentz capture your hearts with the love stories, MAN WITH A PAST and TRUE COLORS.

And in October, watch for the second two-in-one collection by Barbara Delinsky!

Available wherever Harlequin books are sold.

Back by Popular Demand

Janet Dailey
Americana

A romantic tour of America through fifty favorite Harlequin Presents® novels, each set in a different state researched by Janet and her husband, Bill. A journey of a lifetime in one cherished collection.

In June, don't miss the sultry states featured in:

Title # 9 - FLORIDA
             Southern Nights
     #10 - GEORGIA
             Night of the Cotillion

Available wherever
Harlequin books are sold.

JD-JR

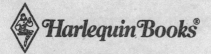 **_Harlequin Books_**®

GREAT NEWS ...

HARLEQUIN UNVEILS NEW SHIPPING PLANS

For the convenience of customers, Harlequin has announced that Harlequin romances will now be available in stores at these convenient times each month*:

Harlequin Presents, American Romance, Historical, Intrigue:

> May titles: April 10
> June titles: May 8
> July titles: June 5
> August titles: July 10

Harlequin Romance, Superromance, Temptation, Regency Romance:

> May titles: April 24
> June titles: May 22
> July titles: June 19
> August titles: July 24

We hope this new schedule is convenient for you.

With only two trips each month to your local bookseller, you'll never miss any of your favorite authors!

*Please note: There may be slight variations in on-sale dates in your area due to differences in shipping and handling.

Harlequin Superromance®

**Here are the longer, more involving stories you
have been waiting for . . . Superromance.**

Modern, believable novels of love, full of the complex
joys and heartaches of real people.

Intriguing conflicts based on today's constantly
changing life-styles.

Four new titles every month.
